'I knew you we... job from the star...

Seth continued savagely, 'You don't look right, you don't dress right and you've absolutely no idea how to behave.'

'B-but what about our agreement?' stammered Daisy.

'Since you haven't stuck by a word of it, I hardly think that you're in a position to quote it back to me now,' he pointed out with a cold look. 'You've been nothing but trouble, and I'm not putting up with you any longer.'

'But you've told everyone that you're in love with me now,' Daisy said desperately.

'I'll find someone else,' Seth said flatly. 'And next time I'll make sure I get a girl who doesn't argue!'

Jessica Hart had a haphazard career before she began writing to finance a degree in history. Her experience ranged from waitress, theatre production assistant and outback cook to newsdesk secretary, expedition PA and English teacher, and she has worked in countries as different as France and Indonesia, Australia and Cameroon. She now lives in the north of England, where her hobbies are limited to eating and drinking and travelling when she can, preferably to places where she'll find good food or desert or tropical rain.

Recent titles by the same author:

PART-TIME WIFE
KISSING SANTA

BRIDE FOR HIRE

BY
JESSICA HART

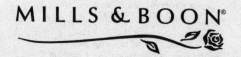

MILLS & BOON®

*First published in Great Britain 1997
Harlequin Mills & Boon Limited,
Eton House, 18-24 Paradise Road, Richmond, Surrey TW9 1SR*

© *Jessica Hart 1997*

ISBN 0 263 80177 2

Set in Times Roman 10½ on 11½ pt.
02-9707-55591 C1

*Printed and bound in Great Britain
by Mackays of Chatham PLC, Chatham*

CHAPTER ONE

DID she dare?

Daisy chewed her bottom lip as she looked from the telephone to the letter in her hand. It was short and enigmatic, the bold black scrawl thrusting itself across the page as if the writer was used to expressing himself in a blunter, less elusive style. '...your name given to me by a mutual acquaintance...believe you might be interested in a proposition I have in mind...someone of your talents and discretion required for a forthcoming trip to the Caribbean...' Daisy's eyes skimmed the letter again, although she knew it by heart, and stopped at that tantalising mention of the Caribbean, just as they had done when she'd first ripped open the envelope—before she had realised that it wasn't addressed to her at all.

'I will be in London from May 19,' the letter had concluded curtly, with the name and telephone number of one of London's most exclusive hotels. 'Call me if you are interested.' It was signed in the same aggressive script: 'Seth Carrington'.

Daisy looked back at the telephone. She didn't recognise the name, although it had a vaguely familiar ring to it, but everything about the letter was suspicious—not least the fact that Seth Carrington wrote like a man used to dictating letters and having them typed immaculately for him. Why had he written this one by hand? If she had any sense she would fold up the letter, put it back in its envelope and return it to the sender with a message saying that it had been opened in error.

But being sensible wouldn't get her to the Caribbean

and it wouldn't help her find Tom. Wiping her palms on
her skirt, Daisy reached for the phone.

'I'd like to speak to Seth Carrington, please,' she said
when she was finally put through to someone who announced herself as Mr Carrington's personal assistant.

'May I ask who's calling?'

Daisy glanced at the top of the letter. 'Dee Pearce,'
she said, wondering if the other girl could hear the lie.

'I'm afraid Mr Carrington is unavailable at the moment.' The voice at the end of the phone was cool with
suspicion. 'Would you care to leave a message?'

Daisy hesitated. What could she say? What would the
unknown Dee be likely to say? In the end, she just left
her number and rang off, feeling depressed. That the
letter with its prospect of the Caribbean had arrived at
4 Lawrence Crescent instead of 4 Lawrence Street had
been a mere coincidence, but when she had discovered
that Dee Pearce had gone away without leaving a for-
warding address Daisy had been sure that fate was taking
a hand.

That's when the idea had first come to her, but it had
still taken her all night to work up the courage to telephone Seth Carrington and he might at least have had
the decency to be there! Daisy didn't think she would
have the nerve to try again.

The whole idea was madness, anyway, she told herself, slumping down into a chair. It was pretty obvious
that whatever Seth Carrington's *interesting proposition*
was it wasn't going to be anything her mother would be
likely to approve of, and while Daisy was prepared to
do almost anything to find Tom at the moment there
were limits. She would just have to find some other way
to get to the Caribbean to look for him. Seth Carrington
would never ring back, anyway.

The phone rang.

Daisy jumped, her heart hammering as she jerked upright. It was her mother, she persuaded herself as she took a deep breath to calm herself. Her mother or Lisa or Robert, but her palm was still slippery as she picked up the receiver.

'Hello,' she said warily.

'This is Seth Carrington.' It was an American voice, deep and gravelly, with a harsh edge of impatient authority. He sounded just like his writing. 'Is that Dee Pearce?'

Daisy teetered on the brink of indecision, conscious that this was the point of no return. She could say, No, I'm sorry, I've wasted your time; it's all a mistake. That was the only sensible thing to say, and she had every intention of saying it until she opened her mouth and somehow 'Yes,' came out instead.

He had caught the momentary hesitation, though. 'You don't sound very sure,' he commented, and something about the sarcastic tone put Daisy's back up.

'Yes, I'm Dee Pearce,' she lied coldly. 'You took me by surprise, that's all.'

'Easily surprised, aren't you?' said Seth Carrington in the same hatefully sardonic voice. 'You only asked me to ring you five minutes ago. Don't say you've forgotten already?'

'Of course not,' said Daisy. Conscious of being forced onto the defensive, she opted for attack. 'I thought you weren't supposed to be available at the moment,' she went on, matching his sarcastic tone. 'Your secretary certainly gave me the impression that you were far too busy to go anywhere near a phone so, naturally, I wasn't expecting you to call back right away.'

The brief silence at the other end of the phone indicated that Seth Carrington wasn't used to being answered back. 'Maria's there to filter out unwanted calls,' he said after a moment. 'I didn't tell her about you. I'm sure you'll agree that the fewer people who know about you the better.'

'Absolutely,' agreed Daisy, mystified.

'And now, since I *am* extremely busy, perhaps we could get down to business?' he continued brusquely. 'I take it Ed has explained the situation to you?'

Ed? Who was Ed? 'I've just had your letter,' she said cautiously.

Seth swore under his breath. 'He said he'd ring you before he went back to the States,' he said, and Daisy breathed a sigh of relief. If Ed knew Dee Pearce it was just as well he was going to be on the other side of the Atlantic.

'There was a rather vague message on my answering machine,' she said, rather surprised at her own capacity for invention. 'Perhaps he couldn't get hold of me and didn't want to leave too explicit a message.'

Seth only grunted. 'I don't want to explain over the phone. You'd better come up here.' He was clearly thinking aloud. 'I may as well take a look at you, anyway.' There was a sound of impatiently rustled papers. 'I've got a window at four o'clock. Can you make it by then?'

Daisy reflected that she had had more gracious invitations, but this wasn't the time to object to Seth Carrington's telephone manner. If this was a job that took her to the Caribbean then surely it was worth putting up with a little rudeness. 'Yes, I can be there.'

She wasn't surprised when he refrained from going into raptures of delight. 'Don't be late,' was all he said and then added, just before he put the phone down on her, 'And be discreet.'

Daisy was left holding the receiver buzzing in her ear. She put it down slowly, hardly able to believe what she had done. Had that really been her, Daisy Deare—whose most foolhardy adventure to date had been driving through a red light on a deserted street at two in the morning—calmly agreeing to meet a strange man in a hotel to discuss a suspicious-sounding proposition?

For a moment she was tempted not to go, and then she thought of her stepfather, grimly hanging onto life in his hospital bed; of her mother's haggard face, and the guilt in her eyes whenever she thought about Tom. Daisy knew that her mother was convinced that Tom had left because of her, and they both knew that what Jim Johnson wanted more than anything was to see his son again before he died. If they could find him.

Daisy had been in touch with any of Tom's friends that she could think of, but only one had had any news of him. Mike had written to Daisy from Florida, saying that he had last seen Tom on his way down to work in the Caribbean and that he would try to find out more. It had been his letter that Daisy had been expecting when she had snatched up the envelope with the American stamp and ripped it open eagerly, to find herself reading Seth Carrington's enigmatic letter to Dee Pearce.

This was her only chance to get to the Caribbean and find Tom for herself, Daisy reminded herself as she caught the bus into Mayfair. She couldn't come to that much harm in a famous hotel, surely, with that efficient-sounding secretary sitting just outside the door? She could at least hear what Seth Carrington's proposition was. If he was just looking for a call-girl she would simply walk away, but his manner on the phone had been too brusque for that. Why bother with a letter or holding out the lure of a trip to the Caribbean if it was simply a question of sex? Surely there must be easier ways to arrange it?

Besides, Daisy reasoned, Seth Carrington hadn't

sounded like a man who would need to buy women. The fresh green branches of May brushed against the top deck of the bus in the King's Road, but Daisy didn't even notice. Her dark blue eyes were thoughtful as she gazed unseeingly through the window at the shops and the cars and the crowds, and wondered what Seth Carrington would be like. He hadn't been exactly charming on the phone, she thought, remembering that deep, hard voice. 'Ruthless' was the word that slid insidiously into her mind but Daisy dismissed it, along with the tiny shiver creeping down her spine. He probably just had an unfortunate telephone manner.

There was an expensive hush in the hotel foyer. Daisy felt horribly conspicuous in her long black T-shirt and grey leggings as she waited for the lift up to the penthouse suite. Everyone else looked so sleek and glamorous with that indefinable sheen of wealth. She was passionately grateful that the lift was empty when it arrived. She could study her own wide-eyed reflection in the mirror as she slid silently upwards, and reflected that if Seth Carrington was expecting her to look sleek and glamorous he was in for a disappointment.

Her mop of dark curls looked tangled no matter how firmly she brushed them and, although she was slender, she had a sort of gangly awkwardness that could never in a million years be confused with sleekness. No, she would never be glamorous, Daisy sighed to herself, surveying her heart-shaped face with its merry mouth and innocent blue eyes beneath tilted lashes. She looked young, fresh, even pretty, but definitely not glamorous.

She would never get away with it! In a sudden surge of panic Daisy reached out to press the button to take her back down to the ground floor, but it was too late. The lift doors were whispering open, and a svelte assistant was rising from behind a desk to greet her. In her late thirties, she had a mask-like expression that didn't quite conceal her surprise at the sight of Daisy in her leggings.

'Mr Carrington still has a visitor with him,' she said. 'He won't keep you long. Would you like to take a seat?'

What she would really like to do was go home and forget that she had ever seen the name, Seth Carrington. Instead, Daisy perched on the edge of one of the plush sofas and bolstered her confidence with the thought that he had no way of knowing that she wasn't Dee Pearce and that, even if he had, the worst he could do was tell her to get out.

Suddenly the door on the far side of the room opened with the force of a slap and Daisy's heart jumped to her throat. Even if she hadn't heard his voice as he said goodbye to his guest she would have known instantly which of the two men was Seth Carrington. He was dark and very powerfully built, with a harsh face and a quality of almost overwhelming magnetism. Escorting his guest to the lift, he shook his hand and waited until the doors had closed after him before he turned and a steely stare swung round to Daisy, who was still perched nervously on the sofa and feeling completely out of place.

Without quite knowing why, she got to her feet. 'Hello.' Her voice came out as a thin squeak, and she cleared her throat in embarrassment.

His brows rose and then snapped together. 'Dee Pearce?'

Daisy didn't like the incredulous note in his voice, but she nodded. 'Yes,' she said, and his frown deepened. She thought for a moment that he was going to tell her to get out there and then but, after an unnervingly hard look, he strode over and held the door open for her.

'You'd better come in,' he said, and then glanced over

at his secretary. 'Hold all calls, Maria.' He stood back as Daisy passed him, peeking a nervous glance up at his forbidding expression under her lashes. She wished now that she'd run while she'd had the chance.

Seth shut the door behind her and Daisy found herself in a luxuriously appointed living area with several doors leading off it. It was impossible to concentrate on the furnishings, though, with Seth prowling round her like a tiger and looking her up and down with a tiger's baleful stare. More than ever, Daisy wanted to turn and run but the feeling that he was half expecting her to do just that made her tilt up her chin and stare back at him.

There was a flicker of something that might almost have been appreciation in his eyes, and then he pointed at an armchair. 'Sit down.'

'Please,' Daisy muttered under her breath, but she did as she was told.

Then she wished that she hadn't. Sunk into the comfort of the chair, she was at an immediate disadvantage when Seth didn't sit down but towered over her—frowning down at her in a way that made her shift uncomfortably.

'Is something the matter?' she asked at last when he still didn't say anything. He wasn't a conventionally handsome man, she decided, but there was something darkly, dangerously attractive about him. Daisy wasn't quite sure where it lay. Everything about him spoke of arrogance and power. His eyes were the cold colour of iron beneath that alarming frown, the angles of his face fierce and unyielding and his mouth utterly ruthless. Too late Daisy realised that she was staring at it, and her stomach contracted in an odd mixture of apprehension and fascination.

'I was just trying to decide what you were doing here,' Seth said slowly at last, his American drawl very pronounced. It was odd that a voice so deep could sound so cold.

Daisy tore her eyes away from his face and tried to pull herself together. 'You asked me to come,' she said a little uncertainly. 'Don't you remember? We are going to discuss your proposition.'

'I was going to discuss my proposition with Dee Pearce,' he said flatly. 'I want to know who you are.'

'I am Dee,' said Daisy, but she knew that she was beginning to look hunted.

'I don't think so.' Seth propped himself against a table and folded his arms, surveying Daisy with sardonic grey eyes. 'Ed described Dee to me as a stunning blonde.' His cold gaze swept over her dismissively. 'Even allowing for Ed's undoubted talent for exaggeration, I wouldn't have said that description fits you, would you?'

Daisy bit her lip. Why couldn't Dee Pearce have been dark and ordinary-looking? She wondered if it was worth claiming that she always wore a wig whenever she met Ed, but a glance at Seth's implacable mouth made her abandon that idea. He was quite capable of telling her that a wig wouldn't be enough to make her stunning.

'Probably not,' she sighed reluctantly, and was astonished to see a gleam of amusement dissolve the coldness in the grey eyes, transforming his expression for a brief, unnerving instant before they shuttered once more.

'If you're not Dee Pearce, who are you?'

'My name's Daisy Deare,' she said, and saw his brows lift in inevitable mockery. 'That's Deare with an ''e'',' she added with dignity.

'Well, Daisy Dear-with-an-''e'',' he said sardonically, 'perhaps you'd like to explain what you're doing here under false pretences?'

Daisy was thinking fast. 'I'm a friend of Dee's,' she said. 'She...she'd already arranged to go away for three months when she got your letter, but she knew how much I wanted to go to the Caribbean so she suggested I come in her place. We…er…we often help each other out.'

'Do you now?' Daisy didn't like the unpleasant note in Seth's voice. She had a nasty feeling that he hadn't believed a word. 'And are you an actress, too, Daisy *Deare*?'

'Yes,' said Daisy firmly. She hadn't performed in public since a humiliating appearance as a sweet pea in an end-of-term ballet, aged seven, but she was beginning to suspect that Dee Peace didn't spend that much time on stage either. 'Only I'm resting at the moment, so I could go to the Caribbean whenever you wanted.'

Seth ignored that hint. 'Why didn't you tell me this when I called?' he asked abruptly.

'I thought it would be easier to explain face to face. Besides,' she went on with an ingenuous look, 'you might not have agreed to see me if I hadn't said I was Dee.'

'I wouldn't,' Seth told her grimly. 'I only approached Dee in the first place because Ed assured me she was very discreet, and now I find that she gaily passes on my letter to the first out-of-work actress she comes across who fancies a trip to the Caribbean!'

'She wouldn't have told me if she hadn't known that I was discreet too,' said Daisy, who was surprising herself with her own facility for lying. 'Anyway,' she went on frankly, 'I don't know anything to be indiscreet *about* yet. Your letter was as clear as mud! But it sounded as if you needed someone who was uncommitted and, since Dee couldn't make it, I'd have thought you'd have been pleased that she arranged for someone suitable to come instead.'

'I might have been if she *had* sent someone suitable,'

he snapped. 'As it is, you're the exact opposite of what I had in mind. I need someone sophisticated and glamorous.' The cold gaze raked disparagingly from her soft, tousled curls down to her grey leggings and the faded yellow canvas shoes she wore with them. 'You don't look much more than a schoolgirl!'

'I'm twenty-three,' said Daisy, ruffled by that insultingly impersonal scrutiny. 'And I may not look very glamorous at the moment but that's because *you* told me to look discreet, if you remember!'

'It's possible to look discreet without looking like Orphan Annie,' Seth retorted. It was stuffy in the room and he shrugged off his jacket as he straightened, tossing it over the arm of a sofa before prowling round the back of the sofa and over to the window. It was open to the early summer sunshine, and Daisy could hear the traffic grumbling down Park Lane. He stood, looking down at it, for a moment then turned back to Daisy. 'From what I hear about Dee—if you're a friend of hers I imagine that those big blue eyes of yours aren't as innocent as they look, but I doubt that anyone would believe for a minute that I was seriously interested in you.'

Daisy didn't know whether to feel relieved or offended. 'Is that what you want?'

'I need a decoy.' Seth was unbuttoning his cuffs, loosening his tie and rolling up the sleeves of his pale blue shirt, the relaxed intimacy of his actions at odds with his brisk tone. 'I may as well tell you what this is about and then you'll appreciate why you're not suitable, but you'd better be as discreet as you say you are.'

'Of course,' she said, resenting his tone.

'All right, then.' He came back and flung himself into a chair opposite her, obviously working out how he could tell her as little as possible. 'I'm thinking of getting married,' he began.

Whatever Daisy had been expecting, it wasn't that. She stared at him, conscious of a quite absurd trace of wistfulness as she wondered what it would be like to marry someone like Seth Carrington; to see that hard face soften with love. Of course *she* wouldn't want to. So far he had shown himself to be brusque, arrogant and downright unpleasant. He was the last kind of man she would want to marry. On the other hand, it *would* be nice to be able to confide all your problems to someone so strong and patently capable of dealing with them... Seth Carrington looked like a man who would guard his own, unlike Robert who was always so infuriatingly understanding about everything.

With a jerk, Daisy recalled herself to the present. 'Er...congratulations,' she offered, not at all clear what her own role in all of this was to be.

Seth looked faintly exasperated at her reaction, and she wondered if he suspected her of being sarcastic. 'I've managed to avoid marriage up to now,' he said repressively, 'but Astra is a very special lady, and our companies complement each other. Marriage would be an ideal merger in every way.'

Daisy regarded him with puzzled blue eyes. He sounded pretty cool about the whole idea. Anyone would think that the business merger interested him more than his future wife, no matter what he might say about her being a special lady. Then another thought occurred to her and she sat up. It wasn't exactly a common name...'Astra?'

'Astra Bentingger.'

'*Astra Bentingger*?' Daisy's voice rose to a squeak. Astra Bentingger had inherited one of the largest fortunes in the world at the age of eighteen but, far from being crushed by the responsibility, she had taken her vast business into her own capable hands and made herself even richer. Barely a week went by without her picture appearing in some newspaper or magazine. Clever, effortlessly beautiful, fluent in five languages, known and courted and gossiped about the world over, Astra Bentingger was a name to conjure with. The original Superwoman, thought Daisy glumly, intimidated by the mere idea of her.

She looked at Seth with a touch of awe. If he was contemplating marriage with Astra Bentingger he must be even richer and more powerful than she had thought at first. It was well known that Astra only liked men who played in the same league… 'But isn't she—' Daisy broke off as she remembered where she had last read about Seth's fiancée. 'Married to Dimitrios Klissalikos?' he finished for her, unperturbed. 'Yes, she is. That's part of the problem.'

'I can see that already having a husband might be a bit of a drawback if she's contemplating marrying you,' said Daisy.

Seth's brows drew together at her facetiousness. 'Naturally, Astra will be obtaining a divorce, but we're still negotiating a pre-nuptial contract and for the moment we have to be extremely careful that our names aren't linked at all. That's where Dee came in. I need to be seen around with someone else to divert attention from my relationship with Astra. For the time being, I'll only appear to meet her in large parties while the press think I'm involved with someone quite different—someone who's prepared to act the part of a besotted girlfriend.

'A friend of mine met Dee when he was over here last year and, when I mentioned the matter to him, he said she'd be ideal. I gather that she's not much of an actress but she's apparently stunning enough to be a likely girlfriend and, quite apart from being discreet, has the other undoubted advantage of being prepared to do anything for money.'

Seth paused and looked across at Daisy, who was listening with her wide, dark eyes and clear face. 'Are *you* the kind of girl who'd be prepared to do anything for money, Daisy Deare?'

She looked wary. 'Almost anything,' she said and, to her consternation, the unsettling amusement chased across his face again, warming his eyes, lightening the fierce lines of his face and lifting the corners of his mouth in a way that made Daisy wonder desperately what he would look like if he really smiled. Astra would know.

'Very wise,' he said. 'You're obviously the cautious type. No doubt you appreciate now why you wouldn't be an adequate substitute for the real Dee Pearce?'

Daisy saw her chance of finding Tom in the Caribbean slipping away from her. 'I don't see why,' she said stubbornly. 'It seems to me that all you want is someone to hang on your arm at a few parties. I could do that. If you're going to marry Astra Bentingger it's not as if you would want...you know...'

'Sex?' Seth was clearly not a man to waste time on euphemisms. 'No, if I'd wanted a call-girl I could get one easily enough, but I'm not reduced to buying women yet.'

'What's the pre-nuptial contract about, then?' asked Daisy tartly, irritated by his arrogance.

For a moment she wondered if she had gone too far. Seth's eyes bored into hers and his mouth tightened ominously but, to her relief, he decided to let her unwise remark pass. 'What I *want* is a girl who can put on a convincing performance,' he said in a gritty voice. 'I want a girl who can act as if she's in love with me without getting prudish or involved in messy emotions.

A girl who will take the money and disappear discreetly as soon as Astra's divorce comes through in a couple of months. A girl who looks like the kind of girl I might fall in love with...and I wouldn't have said that you'd fit into any of those categories.'

Was he being deliberately insulting or was he just naturally rude? 'I'm only interested in the money,' said Daisy with a frosty look. 'I can assure you that I'm not in the least likely to fall in love with you myself, if that's what you were worrying about.'

'Why not? If it's money you're interested in I ought to be just your type.'

Really, the arrogance of the man was unbelievable! 'I've already got a boyfriend,' she said coldly, mentally crossing her fingers and thinking of the ever-hopeful Robert. 'He's much more my type than you are!'

Seth's steel eyes had sharpened. 'What does that mean?'

'It means he's kind and considerate and not so puffed up with his own importance that he thinks every girl he meets is going to fall in love with him!' The words were out before Daisy could stop herself. Aghast, she cursed her quick temper but after one frozen moment, to her astonishment and intense relief, Seth threw back his head and laughed.

Daisy's bones felt suddenly weak and she was glad that she was sitting down. Relief, she told herself firmly. Nothing whatsoever to do with the effect of his laugh or the way his cheeks creased when he smiled. Nothing to do with the whiteness of his teeth or the extraordinary way he had changed into someone younger, warmer and more approachable—someone disastrously attractive.

'You've got a nerve, I'll give you that,' said Seth, speculation replacing the lingering amusement in his eyes. He got abruptly to his feet. 'Stand up,' he ordered.

If anything, Daisy was grateful to see the return of the old arrogance. It helped to remind her that Seth Carrington was not a good man to start finding attractive. Taking a firm hold on herself, she tilted her chin in unconscious hauteur.

He sighed. 'Stand up, *please*.'

Daisy stood, relieved to find that her knees would hold her after all. Eyes narrowed, Seth walked round her as if she were a car he was considering buying. At any moment she expected him to ask her mileage or demand to see under her bonnet, and she couldn't help stiffening under his critical inspection.

'Maybe you've got some potential after all,' he admitted grudgingly. 'Properly dressed, we might be able to make something of you. Different from my usual style, of course, but that might be no bad thing.' He came to a halt in front of her, studying her fine-boned faced with a frown. 'Why are you so keen to do this?' he asked brusquely.

Daisy considered telling him the truth, but she didn't think that Seth Carrington would want to get involved in her family problems. He was the kind of man who only understood one thing. 'I need the money,' she said badly. It was true, anyway. She certainly couldn't afford to get to the Caribbean any other way.

'Hmm.' Seth began his unnerving prowl once more. He even moved like a big cat, with that easy but somehow deliberate tread and the sense of a coiled strength which was liable to explode into action at any moment. 'What about this boyfriend of yours? What's he going to think when he sees pictures of you out with me?'

'I'll explain everything to him, of course. Naturally, once he knows that there's no question of us sleeping together he'll understand.' Privately Daisy thought that Robert would be appalled at the very idea but, in spite of his years of dogged devotion, she had never given him any reason to think that she thought of him as anything other than an old friend.

'Will he?' Seth's expression was saturnine. 'I wouldn't let a girl of mine go out with another man, no matter what she told me.'

'Given that your girl is currently married to another man, I hardly think that puts you in a position to criticise Robert,' flashed Daisy, and Seth's eyes narrowed dangerously once more.

'If you want this job you're going to have to learn to hold that tongue of yours,' he said softly. '*Do* you want it?'

Daisy decided that she had said quite enough. She nodded.

'If it wasn't for the fact that I haven't the time to start chasing over London for someone more suitable I'd be tempted to tell you what you and your paragon of a boyfriend could do together,' he went on in the same menacingly quiet voice. 'Unfortunately your need and mine seem to coincide, so it looks as if I'm going to have to make the best of a bad job.' He scowled at the thought and sat on the arm of the sofa. 'Are you sure you can act?'

She was going to get away with it! He was going to take her to the Caribbean after all! Giddy relief lit up Daisy's face. 'Oh, yes,' she said breezily.

Seth didn't appear entirely convinced. 'Well, let's have an audition, shall we?'

'An audition?' Daisy's grin faltered. 'What sort of audition?'

'You haven't been giving a very good impression of a girl in love so far, have you?' he pointed out caustically. 'I want to know if you can convince other people that you've only got eyes for me.'

'What do you want me to do?' she asked warily.

He shrugged. 'Pretend there's someone else in the room. How would you show that you were in love with me?'

'I probably wouldn't if there was someone else in the room!'

'You're going to have to do better than that, Daisy,' he snorted. 'I'm not going to pay you to stand around being all English and repressed. Pretend that you don't know anyone else is watching if that makes it any easier!'

'Oh, all right!' Grumbling, Daisy walked over to where he was still sitting on the arm of the sofa. It was easier without him towering over her, but when she got close to him her nerve failed her. She stopped. Seth folded his arms and looked blandly back at her.

'Well?'

She was going to have to do something. Daisy edged a little closer and reached out a hand to touch his face. His skin was warm and brown, slightly rough, and her fingers tingled so much at the feel of it that she withdrew her hand sharply.

'Is that it?' Seth's acid question jerked her back to herself and she was conscious of a spurt of anger. He was making this deliberately difficult so that she would give up the whole idea! Well, she wasn't gong to! She was going to go out to the Caribbean and she was going to find Tom, and if it meant kissing Seth Carrington then that's what she would do!

With an abrupt movement, Daisy placed herself firmly between his knees and put her hands on Seth's shoulders. She could feel the strength of his muscles and the warmth of his skin through the fine cotton of his shirt. Propped against the sofa arm as he was, his head was almost on a level with hers. For a long moment blue eyes looked into inscrutable grey and then, before her courage failed her again, she leant slowly forward and touched her lips to the pulse that beat at the angle of his jaw and throat.

CHAPTER TWO

DAISY'S lips were soft against the firmness of Seth's jaw and she could smell the clean, masculine scent of his skin with its faintly expensive tang of aftershave. Without intending to, Daisy found her mouth lingering against him. There was something irresistibly solid about him—something magnetising, something tantalising—something that made her drift her lips in feather-light kisses below his ear.

Seth's arms were still folded in front of him and he stayed utterly still beneath her touch, his very lack of response a provocation. Piqued, Daisy began to press slow, enticing kisses along his jaw instead. She had forgotten her intention to withdraw after that first token touch to his throat. She had forgotten that she hardly knew this man; forgotten that what she did know she didn't like; forgotten everything but the feel of his skin like tempered steel beneath her lips and her determination to make him acknowledge the simmering awareness in her kisses.

Slowly, slowly, she worked her way along his jaw, but it wasn't until she reached the tantalising corner of his mouth that she felt his lips begin to curl upwards in an equally slow smile. 'Go on,' he said, but the steadiness in his voice made Daisy pause. She made as if to withdraw but he had unfolded his arms at last and his hands were at her waist, drawing her back against him, and suddenly it seemed the most natural thing in the world to melt into him and feel his lips part beneath hers.

They fitted against each other perfectly. Somehow she had expected Seth's mouth to feel as cold and calculating as it looked, but it wasn't. It was warm, warmer than Daisy would have believed possible as they kissed and then kissed again. A gathering excitement looped around them, tightening its coils around them until the only thing to do was to relax into it and slide her arms from his shoulders around his neck to stop herself being swept away altogether.

She was bewitched, intoxicated by the sweet persuasion of his lips and the unyielding hardness of his body as he held her against him, and when his hands slid beneath her T-shirt to spread possessively over her skin Daisy's only response was to murmur low in her throat and arch her back into his touch. His fingers were searing, making her gasp as they explored her slenderness and drifted insistently upwards to curve around her breast.

It was that sharp intake of breath at the jolt of electric excitement that broke the kiss. Daisy found herself staring down into unreadable grey eyes, her own dazed and very blue, and then Seth slid his hands back to her waist to put her from him with something which might have been reluctance.

'That was very good, Daisy Deare,' he said, his breathing still slightly ragged. 'That was really very good indeed. It seems that you can act, after all.'

Daisy was so shaken that she could hardly stand. Her legs felt insubstantial, as if she were held up by no more than the frantic flutter of a thousand butterfly wings. She couldn't believe what she had done. Had that really been she, arching beneath the touch of a perfect stranger; sinking into his kiss; abandoning herself to the shivery thrill of his lips and his hands? Appalled at herself, she swallowed hard and fought to steady her own voice.

'It's amazing what you have to do to get a job now, isn't it?' It was barely more than a croak but at least she managed to get a whole sentence out, which was a miracle under the circumstances.

Seth's cool gaze rested for a moment on the huge blue eyes before dropping to her mouth which was still burning from his touch. 'I think I can say that you've passed your audition with flying colours—if you still want the job, that is?'

She wasn't going to go through that to give up the job now! Daisy's chin lifted a fraction. 'Yes.' Her voice wasn't quite steady yet, but with every moment she was getting a better grip on herself. 'Why else would I have kissed you?'

'Why, indeed?' Seth got up from the sofa, his grey eyes sardonic. 'I just hope poor old Robert is as understanding as you say he is. Does he know just how well you "act", Daisy?'

'Does Astra Bentingger know how thoroughly you audition?'

Seth's expression was flinty as he took Daisy's chin in one strong brown hand. 'I've warned you before about that tongue of yours, Daisy,' he said and, although she met his eyes bravely, inwardly Daisy quailed at his tone. 'Do you want to learn what I'm like when I'm pushed too far?'

One look into his eyes was enough to give her the answer to that. Daisy moistened her lips. 'No.'

'In that case, I suggest that you learn to keep your tongue firmly between your teeth.' He released her face and Daisy stepped back, resisting the urge to rub her chin where he had held her. It was impossible to imagine that only minutes ago she had twined her arms around this formidable man's neck and quivered with excitement at his kisses. 'Astra is none of your business,' Seth went on coldly. 'As far as I'm concerned, you're going to be working for me just like any other employee. That means you get paid to do as you're told, not to be smart. Is that understood?'

'Perfectly.'

He gave her a hard look then moved away, suddenly brisk. 'All right, let's get down to business. The deal is that you agree to act as my girlfriend until Astra's divorce comes through or until such time as I decide that there's no need to keep up the pretence any longer. It means you'll have to spend at least the next few weeks with me, but in return I'm prepared to pay you a considerable sum of money—in cash—to ensure your discretion.'

Daisy's jaw dropped when Seth told her just how much he would pay her. 'Is that acceptable?' he asked, turning to frown at her gaping expression.

Acceptable? Daisy had never even contemplated having such a large sum of money before! It would at least take the immediate burden of financial worries off her mother's shoulders, she calculated quickly. 'I think so,' she said, pursing up her lips and trying to look as if she discussed sums like that every day of the week. 'That sounds fine.'

'You'll get paid at the end,' Seth warned her, 'when you've shown me that you can behave.'

Daisy was still trembling inside from the effect of his kiss, but she managed to move away quite coolly. 'We will go to the Caribbean?'

'Yes, I've invited a number of guests to my island as a cover for meeting Astra there.'

'Your *island*?'

He raised an eyebrow. 'Is there a problem?'

'I thought you might have a house there,' said Daisy. 'I didn't think you'd have a whole island!'

One of those unsettling gleams of amusement sprang to the grey eyes. 'It's only a small island, if that makes you feel any better.'

'Does that mean we'll be stuck out on our own, or will we be able to get to the other islands?' Daisy asked anxiously, and his brows lifted.

'Being "stuck out on our own" is generally the idea behind having your own island,' he pointed out with some acidity. 'But if you're desperate for crowds we can take the seaplane or one of the boats. Where did you want to go?'

Mike had recommended that Daisy started looking in the Windward Islands, but it had only been one of the places Tom had mentioned. 'I was just wondering,' she said vaguely. She had no idea how she was going to start looking for Tom, but there was no point in worrying about it until she got there. Anyway, with the kind of money Seth was offering, she would be able to afford to travel around if necessary, Daisy reminded herself buoyantly. 'When are we going?' she asked Seth, who glanced at her suspiciously.

'You seem very keen to get to the Caribbean, Daisy.'

'I've always wanted to go there, that's all.' For some reason, Daisy was reluctant to tell Seth about Tom and her stepfather's illness. He was too ruthless, too calculating—the kind of man who would be impatient of sentiment and messy emotions—and if he thought that Daisy's mind wasn't going to be entirely on the job she knew that he would have no compunction in calling off the whole deal. There would be no point in appealing to Seth's better nature. Daisy doubted very much that he even had one.

Look at the chilly way he was approaching his marriage with Astra Bentingger, and any man who could kiss like that and remain totally unmoved had to be ut-

terly heartless. No, better by far to let him think that she
was an impoverished actress, desperate for a palm-
fringed beach.

'Well, if you're planning on island-hopping you're
going to have to wait until I've finished with you,' said
Seth, unwittingly demonstrating his overbearing image.
'I'm not having you jaunting off when I need you on
hand to look suitably adoring.'

'How long do you think that'll be?'

'A month? Six weeks? Maybe longer.' He quirked a
sardonic eyebrow at her. 'Think Robert will be able to
manage without you that long?'

'I expect so,' said Daisy with a frosty look. She didn't
like the sneer in Seth's voice whenever he mentioned
Robert. Robert might not be very exciting, but at least
he had a kind heart.

'He'd better start getting used to it right away,' said
Seth callously. 'I've got a number of social engagements
over the next couple of weeks and, if we're going to
establish you as my girlfriend, we may as well start tonight. I'll take you out to dinner.'

He walked over to the door, as if to indicate that the
interview was now over, while Daisy eyed him resentfully. She had been planning to visit Jim in hospital that
evening. The brusque way Seth gave orders and arrogantly assumed that everyone else would fall in with
them without question riled her. She stayed stubbornly
where she was.

'What if I've got other plans for this evening?'

'Cancel them,' said Seth with insulting indifference
and opened the door. 'If you give Maria your address
I'll come and pick you up at eight o'clock.'

Daisy tried to imagine Seth turning up at her front
door. He would look completely alien in their quiet
south London street and, quite apart from anything else,

it wouldn't take him long to work out that her address was too close to Dee Pearce's for coincidence. 'There's no need for you to collect me,' she said quickly. 'I'll come here.'

'What's the matter, Daisy?' mocked Seth. 'Don't you want Robert to meet your new boss?'

'I'd rather keep my private life entirely separate,' said Daisy, trying—and failing—to sound quelling. Seth certainly didn't appear noticeably quelled.

'Just make sure you're looking a bit smarter than you do now,' was all he said, and nodded unmistakably at the door. 'Now beat it,' he said. 'I've got work to do.'

Daisy bridled at his dismissal all the way home. He was insufferably rude, infuriatingly overbearing, unbelievably arrogant! There she was—prepared to humiliate herself by pretending to actually *like* the man and he carried on as if he was doing *her* a favour! Simmering, Daisy glowered out of the window of the bus. She wished she could have told Seth what he could do with his pretence but the thought of Jim, lying in hospital longing for a reconciliation with his son, had held her tongue at the crucial moment and she had had to content herself with stalking past him without a word of farewell.

The next few weeks were not going to be easy, Daisy acknowledged gloomily to herself. There was nothing easy about Seth Carrington. She could picture him with unnerving clarity, as if his image were scorched into her brain—the dark, forbidding lines of his face, the hardness of his eyes, the disturbing set of his mouth.

Daisy shifted uneasily in her seat and the colour surged into her cheeks at the memory of how that mouth had felt against hers. What had possessed her to kiss him like that—to let herself be kissed like that? Why couldn't she have stepped coolly away from him after a token peck on the cheek? That's all it would have taken. Instead, she had taken him at his word and kissed him like a lover, and now she couldn't forget the touch and the taste and the feel of him. It was as if she could still breathe in his scent; still feel the tantalising roughness of his skin beneath her lips.

Somehow, when she had been with Seth, the fact that she had been able to argue with and kiss a perfect stranger within a few minutes of meeting him had seemed perfectly natural, but now that she was away from the overwhelming magnetism of his presence the memory of her odd behaviour struck Daisy with the force of a blow and she sat, appalled, as she realised what she had done. She must have been mad!

Her mother seemed to agree when Daisy gave her a very edited version of her afternoon's activities. 'You went under completely false pretences to see a man you've never met before in your life and agreed to spend the next few weeks posing as his girlfriend?' she summarised incredulously. 'Daisy, what were you thinking of?'

'I was thinking of Jim,' said Daisy, crouching down beside her mother's chair. 'I know it sounds unusual, Mum, but it's just a job. He's not interested in me at all.'

'So he says!'

'He wants to marry someone else—that's the whole point,' said Daisy patiently. 'Really, he couldn't have made it clearer that I'm not his type and he's definitely not mine!' Treacherously her mind veered to that terrible kiss before she managed to wrench it firmly away. 'It's a business arrangement, that's all, and it's the only chance I've got to get to the Caribbean and look for Tom. Think what it would mean to Jim if I could persuade him to come home?'

Ellen Johnson twisted her hands together in her lap. 'If only you could! But Tom never accepted me. I'm sure that's why he left. He wouldn't want to come back, knowing that I was here.'

'He might have resented you at first, but you weren't the reason he and Jim argued,' said Daisy stoutly, as she had said so many times before. 'They were both too stubborn to give in and admit that they needed each other. I'm sure Tom would come back at once if he knew how ill Jim was. That's why I've got to track him down somehow. I know things are busy in the flower shop at the moment, but Lisa can cope if you just keep an eye on things.'

'But what if this girl Dee Pearce turns up?' worried Ellen, still unconvinced by Daisy's breezy assurance that she had found herself a job that would take her to the Caribbean. 'She might tell this man that you're not friends at all, and then what will he think?'

'She won't turn up,' Daisy assured her confidently. 'I told you, Mum. As soon as I realised that the letter wasn't addressed to me at all I took it round to her house to explain why I'd opened it. I rang the bell, but a neighbour told me that Dee had gone away. That's why the whole thing just seemed like fate.'

'You took a terrible risk,' her mother reproached her.

'If it had been some sort of shady deal I'd have just walked out,' she pointed out, more confident now than she had been when the idea had first occurred to her. 'As it is, it's a perfectly straightforward job. It shouldn't be too hard to hang around and look dumb at a few parties, and in return Seth Carrington will take me out to the Caribbean and give me enough money to find Tom. Easy.' Daisy had forgotten her doubts on the bus and was bent on convincing her mother that she had found the perfect solution.

'Seth Carrington?' Ellen looked at her daughter with new foreboding. 'Not *the* Seth Carrington?'

'I'd hate to think that there were two of him,' said Daisy wryly. 'Why?'

'I was just reading about him on my way to the hospital,' said Ellen, getting up to look through the evening newspaper and fold back a page at last to show Daisy an article. 'He doesn't sound like the kind of man you want to get involved with.'

She handed the paper to Daisy, who glanced through the article. The first section reported Seth's arrival in London, reviewing the ruthlessness of his reputation and the phenomenal success of his vast business empire. The second was headed ONE OF THE WORLD'S MOST ELIGIBLE BACHELORS and made much of the way Seth managed to combine financial success with a jet-setting lifestyle. It contained a whole list of beautiful women who had tried and failed to secure a permanent place in his life. Daisy's lips tightened as she read it.

Still determinedly unmarried at thirty-eight, Seth Carrington had obviously made a career of not committing himself. Right at the end there was some gossipy speculation about his relationship with Astra Bentingger ('currently the fourth Mrs Klissalikos'); perhaps they hadn't been as discreet as Seth had claimed.

Daisy lowered the paper with a sinking feeling at the pit of her stomach, but she refused to be intimidated. She wasn't going to give up her plan at this stage. 'I'm not going to get involved with him,' she told her mother with a not entirely convincing air of confidence. 'I'm going to look for Tom. Seth Carrington is merely incidental.'

In spite of her brave words, Daisy couldn't help feeling more than a little nervous as she took the lift back up to the penthouse suite. Was it only that afternoon that she had stood right there and wondered what Seth Carrington would be like? In a few short minutes he had impressed himself on her consciousness so utterly that it was impossible now to remember a time when his forbidding features hadn't dominated her thoughts.

Daisy tugged at the neckline of her dress and pulled a face at the mirror. She had done her best to look smart, but no amount of brushing could make her curls lie neatly and her make-up was limited to lipstick and an inexpert stroke of blusher. Somehow she didn't think that Seth Carrington was going to be very impressed.

He wasn't. 'Is that the best you could do?' he greeted her, opening the door of the suite himself. He was formally dressed in an immaculate dinner jacket and bowtie, and looked so unnervingly, unfairly attractive that Daisy felt quite weak at the knees.

She quelled the feeling sternly. 'Good evening,' she said brightly. 'Yes, I'm fine, thank you. Yes, I *would* like to come in.'

Seth scowled, but stood back to let her into the suite. Maria had gone—no doubt with relief, thought Daisy sourly. Spending a whole day putting up with Seth Carrington's rudeness would be enough to try anybody. 'I thought I told you to wear something smart?' he accused her, shutting the door with a snap.

'What's wrong with my dress?' said Daisy, a little offended. She had expected him to criticise her face, but she had blown her meagre savings on this dress in last summer's end-of-season sales where it had been reduced from some exorbitant price. Everyone had said it had been worth it, though. The dusky blue colour with its pattern of tiny stars suited her dark hair and pale skin, and Daisy had always felt rather good in it...until now.

'It looks as if you've picked it up off some bargain rail,' said Seth dismissively, and her lips tightened.

'Are you always this charming?'

'I can't afford to waste my time tiptoeing around your finer feelings,' he said irritably.

'I can't imagine you tiptoeing around anyone's feelings,' grumbled Daisy, finding it easier to squabble than to notice how devastatingly attractive Seth looked in his dinner jacket. She avoided looking at the sofa where they had kissed, but it kept catching annoyingly at the corner of her eye. 'I've never met anyone so inconsiderate.'

Seth looked nettled. 'I'm perfectly considerate when I need to be but, as I keep having to remind you, you're here to do a job.'

'Yes, and I might find it easier if you weren't quite so unpleasant!'

It was obvious that Seth Carrington wasn't used to being answered back. He glowered at Daisy for a moment and then gave a short, exasperated sigh, not entirely unmixed with amusement. 'Are you always this argumentative?'

'Only when provoked,' said Daisy, assuming a demure expression that didn't fool Seth for a minute.

'Look, I'm merely trying to point out that you don't exactly fit my image.' He eyed her moodily. 'It's not just that the dress looks cheap. It's a good girl's dress—makes you look too unsophisticated. It's well known that my taste is for women with a little more glamour. We'll just have to get you some decent clothes tomorrow.'

Daisy's mind went back to the article her mother had shown her. Seth's name had been linked with any number of famous women, and it had to be said that none of them would have been described as good girls. 'Why can't we convince them that you've changed your image and fallen for a nice girl for a change?'

'That's not very likely, is it?' said Seth with one of his disparaging looks, and Daisy folded her arms huffily.

'You could pretend.'

'I'm paying you to do the pretending, not me,' he pointed out brutally. 'And if you're going to do it effectively you're going to have to dress the part.' He turned away to pick up the phone. 'I'd better cancel our reservation.'

'My dress isn't that bad, is it?' asked Daisy in dismay.

'It is for what I had in mind,' said Seth as he punched out a number. 'I had intended to take you somewhere where we'd be noticed, but I'm not being photographed with you looking like a schoolgirl.' He waited while the phone rang at the other end. 'We'll go somewhere quiet instead tonight.'

Daisy was secretly relieved as the lift slid silently back down to the ground floor. She wasn't sure that she was quite ready to start acting out her role in front of the paparazzi just yet. A sleek black car was waiting outside the hotel entrance and at Seth's appearance a uniformed chauffeur sprang into action, holding open the door for Daisy who sank wide-eyed back into the luxurious seat.

'I've never been in a car like this before,' she confided to Seth after he had given the chauffeur his instructions.

The glance he gave was half puzzled, half amused. 'Don't tell me that air of innocence is real after all?'

Daisy regretted her impulsive remark. She could still remember the look on his face as he had released her. 'Perhaps you can act after all,' he had said. The last thing she wanted was for him to think that she wasn't quite the actress she claimed to be! 'I don't usually travel in such style, that's all,' she said, trying to assume a world-weary air, but she wasn't sure whether Seth was quite convinced. He continued to watch her with a speculative expression until they reached the restaurant.

Any hopes Daisy might have had about popping round the corner to a cheap and cheery Italian were dashed when the car drew up outside one of the most expensive restaurants in London, but at least they were shown to a secluded table and the atmosphere was dark and intimate and positively reeking with discretion. There would be no flashing cameras here.

She opened her menu with enthusiasm. 'I'm starving,' she said, momentarily forgetting her world-weary role. 'I didn't have time for lunch.' Glancing across at Seth, she found him watching her with an oddly arrested look in his eyes and she lowered the menu guiltily. 'Oh, dear, I suppose it's not very sophisticated to be interested in food?'

Seth gave one of his sudden, heart-shaking smiles. 'I won't tell,' he promised. 'It'll be a refreshing change to have a meal with a woman who doesn't just push salad around her plate all evening.'

Trusting that to mean that she would be allowed a pudding as well, Daisy ordered the most substantial starter she could find and then dithered happily over a choice of main course until Seth grew impatient and ordered for her.

'She'll have the lamb,' he said to the waiter, who had been standing there with his pencil patiently poised for some time.

'I was just going to order the poussin,' hissed Daisy indignantly as the waiter removed the menus with admirably concealed relief.

'I thought you were hungry?' he retorted. 'If I hadn't made the decision for you we'd have been here all night.'

Daisy contented herself with muttering under her

breath and buttering her roll with a certain lavish defiance.

'Talking of "all night",' Seth went on, leaning casually back in his chair, 'you'd better move into my suite tomorrow.'

Daisy's head jerked up, knife poised in mid-butter. 'Move in?' she echoed in dismay. 'Why?'

'It's not for that rather nice body of yours which you keep so cleverly concealed beneath those shapeless clothes,' he said with a dryness that sent the colour rushing to her cheeks.

Grateful for the dim light, Daisy reapplied herself to her roll and forced down the treacherous memory of his hands curving around her breasts and sliding down her spine, warm against her skin. 'I don't see why I have to move in with you.'

'Because, Daisy, word will soon get around if I'm seen putting you chastely into a taxi every night and, while you and I may know that we're not going to fall into bed as soon as we get in, we want everyone else to think that we can't keep our hands off each other, don't we?'

'I don't see how anyone's going to know whether we sleep together or not,' grumbled Daisy, who wished that she couldn't imagine the prospect in quite such unnerving detail and was desperately trying to disguise her perturbation with bolshiness. 'Why can't I just sneak out the back way?'

'Someone would be bound to see you and the next thing we'd know there'd be a snippet in the gossip columns, speculating about just how close our relationship was.'

'But who cares what we do?' cried Daisy. 'Who on earth is going to be interested in what time I go home?'

Seth shrugged. 'You'd be surprised. I'm afraid it's one

of the drawbacks of fame. People seem to think that as soon as you acquire money or influence you forfeit your right to privacy. It's something you're just going to have to get used to over the next few weeks. If no one was interested in me or Astra there wouldn't be any need for you to be here at all, so you can thank the gossip columns for your job…and your job is living with me for the moment.'

'Will…?' She hesitated, cleared her throat and tried to sound unconcerned. 'We won't have to share a bed as well, will we?'

'No.' Seth's eyes gleamed with ironic understanding. 'There's another room in the suite. Maria's been using it, but she's going to stay with friends so she won't need it. She'll come in during the day, but I'll need you to be there, too, so you might as well stay.'

'What do you need me for?' Marginally reassured by the promise of a room to herself, Daisy had just taken a bite of her roll and her voice was rather indistinct.

'In case people turn up.' The wine waiter was presenting the bottle for Seth's inspection, and he tasted the wine before giving a cursory nod and turning back to Daisy. 'I've got a number of business meetings scheduled, but other people tend to drop by for one reason or another and that means you being there to prove that I can't bear not to have you at my side.'

'I can't sit around all day just on the off chance that someone's going to drop by,' she protested. 'I'll go potty without anything to do.'

Seth watched the waiter pour the wine into her glass. 'I'd have thought you'd be used to that.'

'What do you mean?' asked Daisy indignantly. Most days she hardly got a chance to sit down at all!

'Being an out-of-work actress,' he explained, raising an eyebrow at her expression. 'I've always imagined that meant sitting by the phone, waiting for the call to stardom.'

She had forgotten that she was meant to be an actress. 'That's the advantage of an answering machine,' she said. Really, she was getting quite good at lying! 'It means I can keep busy.'

'Doing what?' Or can I guess from that very talented performance you gave this afternoon?'

Daisy shot him a hostile look. She didn't want to be reminded about that particular performance. 'Actually, I work in a flower shop,' she said coldly, deciding that it was best to keep as close to the truth as possible. 'When I haven't got a part, that is,' she added, just to remind him of her acting credentials.

'I don't suppose you earn much in a flower shop?' said Seth, who could have bought a whole chain of flower shops without even noticing a blip in his bank balance.

She sighed, thinking of the last difficult year when business had fallen off and the bills had mounted. 'No.'

'I'd have thought a girl with your interest in money would have jumped at the chance of being paid to sit around,' he said in his caustic voice. 'It's not as if it's going to be hard work. There's a television and a health club and, if the worst comes to the worst, you can always read a book.'

'I suppose so,' said Daisy without enthusiasm.

A silence fell. Running her finger around the rim of her glass, Daisy studied the deep golden colour of the wine. She wished that she could stop noticing Seth's hands; wished her eyes would stop following the line of his jaw back to the place below his ear where she had first kissed him. He was drinking his wine, but she could feel his uncomfortably acute gaze on her face and had the sudden, horrible certainty that he knew exactly what she was thinking.

'Have you told Astra about us?' she asked awkwardly. It was the first thing that came into her head as she searched desperately for something to say, but as soon as the words came out she could hear the implied intimacy in that 'us'. 'I mean, have you told her about me?'

Seth's expression was curiously shuttered. 'Yes.'

'What did she say?'

'She was pleased, of course.'

'Oh.' Daisy felt unaccountably put out. 'Did you tell her that I wasn't Dee Pearce?'

'I said that I'd come to an agreement with you instead of Dee,' said Seth. 'I didn't go into details.'

'Didn't she want to know what I was like?' If she had been in love with Seth Carrington she would want to know exactly who he was going to be spending so much time with, Daisy reflected. Perhaps Astra Bentingger knew that she didn't have to worry.

'I told her that you didn't really look right for the part,' said Seth, sounding so bored that Daisy was nettled.

'Did you tell her how I convinced you to give me the part anyway?' she asked sourly, hoping to embarrass him, but she might have known that it was impossible to do that.

Seth merely looked across the table at her, his grey eyes inscrutable. 'I told her that you were a better actress than you looked,' he said. 'I also said that I thought it extremely likely that you'd drive me round the bend but that, having got so far, I'd just have to put up with you.'

CHAPTER THREE

THE disgruntled silence—at least on Daisy's side of the table—was broken by the waiter, arriving with exquisitely presented plates.

Daisy was glad of the excuse to concentrate on her food. She found that she didn't like the idea of Seth coolly discussing her with Astra. Have to put up with her, indeed! No wonder Astra was pleased if he had talked about her like that! Even a superwoman might have a few qualms at the idea of her man pretending to be in love with another girl, but it must have been pretty obvious that Daisy could not even be considered a rival.

Her lobster salad with asparagus was delicious but it might as well have been ashes in Daisy's mouth until she pulled herself together. *She* didn't care what Seth and Astra thought about her. She only wanted to find Tom, and it would be a lot easier if she remembered more often that she was simply here as part of the job.

She glanced across at Seth, who was quite unbothered by her sulky silence. It was easier to look at him when his eyes were on his plate and, as if for the first time, she noted the lines starring the corners of his eyes and the dark hair which was already beginning to show a few strands of grey at the temples. Her gaze was just following the flat, angular planes of his cheeks and the arrogant line of his nose down to his mouth when he looked up unexpectedly and caught her watching him. Daisy's heart gave an odd little somersault as she met that steely, skewering gaze, bumping back into place so abruptly that it left her slightly breathless.

'I...I suppose I should know something about you,' she stammered, not quite sure why she felt the need to explain herself. 'A real girlfriend would know more about you than the fact that you're American and stinking rich.'

'What more do you need to know?' asked Seth sardonically.

'Well...about your family?' Daisy suggested. 'Where you live, what you do...that kind of thing.'

'I never talk about my family,' he said flatly. 'No one will expect you to know anything about them.'

Daisy was longing to ask whether Astra knew, but there was a grim finality in Seth's tone that warned her to steer well clear of the subject. 'What about where you live, then?' she asked instead. 'Or is that a state secret too?'

'I've got several places,' he said indifferently. 'Manhattan, Malibu, Cape Cod, a skiing lodge in Utah...and Cutlass Cay in the Caribbean.'

'But which one's home?'

She could have sworn that Seth had never even considered the question before. He looked momentarily taken aback, then shrugged. 'Wherever I am, I guess.'

'How sad,' she said without thinking, and Seth's brows rose arrogantly.

'Most people wouldn't describe having four luxurious houses to choose from as being a particularly sad situation,' he said stiffly, looking down his nose.

Daisy thought of the unpretentious house in Battersea where she had grown up. Its wallpaper was faded now, its rooms a little shabby and a little cluttered, but it was warm and comfortable and familiar. 'I just think it's sad not to have a place to call home,' she said, her dark blue eyes serious. 'Somewhere you know you belong—with people you love and who love you.'

'I don't believe in love,' said Seth with something of
a sneer, and Daisy looked at him curiously.

'If you think that why are you getting married?'

He didn't answer immediately. Instead, he frowned
down into his glass, swirling the wine around as he
thought. 'Astra and I will make a good team,' he said at
last. 'She's a beautiful woman with a first-class business
brain; we'll be partners as much as anything else. And
we understand each other. Astra isn't sentimental, any
more than I am. Neither of us can afford to be.'

'It's an odd thing not to be able to afford when you
can afford absolutely everything else,' said Daisy. Seth
glanced at her sharply, but she didn't notice. She was
crumbling her roll absently with her knife and wondering
how someone whose kiss was so warm could be content
with such a joyless life. There was something chilling
about his rejection of family, and even marriage with
Astra seemed to be approached from a businesslike point
of view. Daisy had always scoffed at people who
claimed that they wouldn't like to be rich, but she was
beginning to change her mind.

'What about you?' Seth interrupted her thoughts
abruptly. His voice was harsh, almost as if the question
were forced out of him.

Daisy looked up from her roll, surprised. 'Me?'

'I might need to show some awareness of your life
before I met you,' he said, but it sounded oddly like an
excuse.

'But no one's going to be interested in me!' she protested. She couldn't imagine anyone even noticing her
next to Seth.

'You never know,' he said slowly. 'If you were
dressed properly you could be quite taking.'

The possibility of being 'quite taking' didn't compare
well with being described as beautiful with a first-class

business brain, Daisy reflected, piqued. 'I'd have thought that, as far as most people were concerned, the only interesting thing about me is that I'm going to be with you,' she said rather grumpily.

'Perhaps,' Seth agreed, 'but it's always best to be prepared. So, go on. Tell me about yourself.'

'Well…' Daisy hesitated, knowing that her life would seem irredeemably dull to Seth but determined not to make any apologies for it. *She* wasn't the one who looked bleak whenever families were mentioned, after all. 'My father died when I was small, but my mother married again a few years ago and my stepfather's wonderful.' Her voice wobbled a bit when she thought about Jim, who had been so kind to her and brought her mother so much happiness. She *had* to find Tom for him. 'We're a very close family,' she went on more steadily, 'but I can't exactly say that my life has been packed with excitement.'

'Is that why you became an actress?'

'What?' Daisy's eyes slid away as she remembered. 'Oh…yes,' she said hurriedly. 'Yes, I think I hoped I'd find…oh, I don't know…something different. I love my home and my family but sometimes it's all a bit *too* safe.' She stopped, aware that she was giving too much away. It was true, though. She loved creating beautiful displays of flowers but there were times when she longed to escape from the humdrum problems of the shop in Battersea. That was why she had broken with Robert, who was so meticulous and kind but who couldn't understand that she wanted more out of life before she settled down to marriage. Then Jim had fallen ill, and she hadn't thought about excitement for a while.

And now here she was, having dinner with one of the most eligible men in the world who was going to take her off to his own Caribbean island.

Seth had been watching her face. 'So now you're just waiting for a starring role?'

Daisy thought of beautiful, businesslike Astra who was the star of this particular play. She was only the understudy.

'Sort of,' she said with an unconsciously wistful sigh, and there was a tiny moment of silence as they looked at each other.

'Daisy,' Seth began suddenly, but he never finished what he was about to say. A couple had crossed the room towards them, and the man was clapping Seth on the shoulder.

'Seth Carrington! What are you doing here?'

Hardly knowing whether to be relieved or peculiarly disappointed at the interruption, Daisy looked up as well and her eyes widened as she recognised James Gifford-Gould. With his vast inherited fortune and playboy life-style, James was so rarely out of the gossip columns that he was almost familiar. A languid blonde with a cat-like smile hung on his arm and offered her cheek for Seth to kiss as he got to his feet and returned their greetings.

'This is Daisy,' he said, and coolly introduced James and the blonde whose name was Eva.

'Hello,' said Daisy, hoping that she sounded equally composed.

Eva barely nodded. Her eyes had already flickered over Daisy and rested for one disintegrating moment on her dress before quite obviously dismissing her as without interest. James was the sort of man who mentally undressed every female he met, and his eyes lingered rather longer.

'Hel-lo,' he said, his gaze continuing to rove over her. 'You look much too sweet to be with a ruthless type like Seth. 'I didn't think they still made girls like you.' He glanced knowingly at Seth. 'Not your usual style, Seth! Where did you find her?' he joked. 'I'd like one too!'

To Daisy's surprise, Seth was looking boot-faced. 'I'm afraid I got the only one,' he said curtly, 'and I'm keeping her.'

'I quite understand, dear fellow,' said James with a wink. 'I'd feel exactly the same.'

Eva was beginning to look petulant. 'Come *on*, James,' she said, tugging at him, and after a last practised smile at Daisy he allowed himself to be dragged off.

Seth sat down again, scowling. 'That man's the worst gossip in London!'

'Isn't that what you wanted?' said Daisy, puzzled. 'I thought people were supposed to start gossiping about us?'

'Not the way James Gifford-Gould is going to gossip,' said Seth obscurely. He glanced away to where James and Eva were being seated at a table. It was on the other side of the room, but had a clear view of where Seth and Daisy sat. 'Now they'll be watching us all evening,' he grumbled. 'I'll have to act as if I was jealous of the way he looked at you.'

'I thought you were already doing that,' said Daisy with some tartness. She was completely confused about what Seth wanted now!

Seth's expression froze for a moment. 'Why would I be jealous?' he demanded in a glacial voice.

'I can't imagine,' she said frankly, 'but you were giving a pretty good impression of it just now!'

'I was no—' Seth shut his mouth firmly and controlled his temper with an effort. 'Look, we're supposed to be acting like lovers, not arguing. Gifford-Gould won't miss anything!' Reaching across the table, he put his hand over hers and forced a smile. 'It'll be easier if we talk like lovers too. What do lovers talk about?'

'I've no idea,' said Daisy stiffly. She was excruciatingly aware of his hand. It was warm and strong and she could almost swear that the lines in his palm were tingling into her skin.

'Come on, Daisy, you can do better than that! What do you and Robert talk about?'

Daisy had a sudden vision of the last time she had given in to Robert's pleading and agreed to have dinner with him. He had taken a facetious question of hers seriously and spent the rest of the evening explaining to her exactly what a personal equity plan was. Still, it wouldn't do Seth any harm to think that someone loved her, even if she *was* only 'quite taking'!

'Robert and I can talk about anything, 'she assured him, but without quite meeting those acute grey eyes.

'What sort of things?'

'Anything,' Daisy insisted firmly. She tried to withdraw her hand surreptitiously, but Seth's fingers only tightened over hers.

'Oh, no, you don't!' he said. 'You're supposed to be in love with me, remember? If you were in love with me you'd want your hand to stay right where it is, and you'd be talking to *me* about anything!' He bared his teeth at her in a false smile. 'So, go on—start acting as convincingly as you acted this afternoon!'

Daisy's eyes were a dark, hostile blue as they looked into implacable grey, but she managed to force an equally unconvincing smile for the benefit of James and Eva who were, indeed, watching them avidly from the other side of the room. 'I'm sure your experience of lovers is wider than mine,' she said through her teeth, still determinedly smiling. 'What would *you* talk about?'

'If I was in love with you?' Seth considered the question. 'Well, let's see…' He lifted her hand and turned it over between the two of his so that he could trace its outline with his fingers. 'I'd probably tell you all the things I liked about you.'

'That would probably tax your imagination!' said Daisy, trying to sound pert but horribly distracted by the way he was playing with her hand.

'Oh, I don't know. I expect I'd be able to think of something. I could talk about how deep and blue your eyes were, for instance, or how your lashes throw shadows on your cheeks.' He paused; thought some more. 'I might tell you that I loved the way your smile seemed to light up the room or even that stubborn way you tilt your chin when you're cross.'

Daisy swallowed. 'T-that's very good,' she said unevenly. The gravelly voice seemed to be reverberating through her and the warm touch of his hands was making her feel shivery inside. He's just acting, she reminded herself desperately. Like she should be acting. But her throat was dry and her tongue felt stiff and unwieldy, and she could only stare back at him with dark, uncertain eyes.

'And *then*,' Seth went on in the same deep, deep voice, 'I'd probably tell you that I couldn't stop thinking about the way you kissed me; that I kept remembering the feel of your skin and the softness of your lips. And I might kiss your palm, like this.'

He lifted her hand and Daisy felt his mouth press warmly and lingeringly into her palm. The sensation sent a shudder of awareness down her spine and, quite instinctively, her fingers curled against his cheek. Her heart was thumping and thudding with painful insistence, and as she looked at the dark head bent over her hand something twisted inside her so sharply that she caught her breath. Seth lifted his head at that tiny, in-

voluntary gasp and his eyes seemed to reach right into
her heart. 'Would you like to know what I'd do next?'

'W-what?'

'I'd call the waiter over and tell him to forget about
the next course so that we didn't have to wait and I could
take you back to the hotel and spend all night making
love to you.'

Daisy's whole body was booming and strumming and
it was suddenly hard to breathe. Very slowly, Seth lowered her hand onto the table. When she looked down
Daisy found her fingers were curling around his, entwining together as if they had a will of their own.

'Would you come?' Seth asked softly.

She moistened her lips. 'If I were in love with you,'
she whispered, horrified at how cracked and husky her
voice sounded.

'And what would you say if you were?'

'I…I think I might say that no one had ever made me
feel this way before,' said Daisy unevenly. 'I might even
say that I found it scary.'

There was a long silence where nothing existed but
his eyes looking into hers and their fingers tangling together on the pale green tablecloth. And then the waiter
was there—hovering over them, serving the main course
with a flourish and refilling their glasses. Seth looked
blank at his appearance, as if he had momentarily forgotten where he was, and it was a second or two before
he released Daisy's hand. He sat back in his chair, the
old shuttered look dropping back into place.

Her hand felt cold and lost, marooned on the table
until she drew it back onto her lap. She felt jolted and
disorientated and regarded her meal without enthusiasm.

'I thought you were starving?' said Seth, noticing her
pushing her food around her plate.

'I was,' said Daisy whose appetite had entirely deserted her. 'I think my starter must have been very fill-ing.'

Seth sent her a quizzical look but, to her relief, didn't pursue the subject. He seemed to have forgotten the need to impress James and Eva, and a rather constrained silence fell. Daisy's heart was still slamming uncomfortably against her ribs. She looked at her wine; at the light gleaming on the cutlery; at the wax oozing down the candle; at anything, except Seth sitting dark and enigmatic on the other side of the table.

What would it be like if they really were in love? What would it be like to know that when he signalled for the bill he really was going to take her back to his suite and undress her slowly? What would it be like to run her hands over his body and feel him smile against her skin?

Memories of his kiss, of the feel of his lips against her palm, fluttered just below her skin, quivering through her to gather in a hot, throbbing core that made her shift restlessly in her seat. She should be thinking about Tom, about Astra, not about the way Seth's mouth kept catching at the edge of her vision or how right her hand had felt in his.

'Would you like a dessert?' he asked when their plates had been removed at last.

'No. Thank you.'

'Coffee?'

She shook her head.

'In that case, shall we go?'

Everything happened just as Daisy had imagined it. Seth barely lifted a finger and the bill arrived discreetly. Then they were walking towards the door and his hand was warm against her back, but they weren't going to the hotel and they wouldn't make love because this was all just a play and there was no need to perform when they were alone.

'I'll get a taxi,' she said as soon as they got outside.

Seth looked irritated. 'I'll take you home,' he began sharply, but Daisy was already stepping to the curb.

''I'd rather go alone,' she said with a touch of desperation, waving frantically at a black cab which obligingly snapped off its yellow light and veered across the road towards them. It squealed to a halt beside Daisy, and waited, its engine ticking noisily.

Thwarted, Seth reached out and took a firm hold of Daisy's wrist before she could leap into the taxi. 'You might at least say goodnight nicely,' he growled.

'G-goodnight,' said Daisy nervously, but he only tsk-tsked and pulled her against him.

'Not good enough, Daisy,' he said. 'We wouldn't want to disappoint anyone watching us through the window, would we? They'd be expecting me to kiss you, and that's just what I'm going to do.'

One of his hands kept her firmly in place, the other slid beneath the curls to hold the nape of her neck while he bent his head and kissed her. Daisy tried to hold herself rigid, her hands flat against his chest, but she was helpless against the wash of sheer pleasure that swept through her.

This was what she had been thinking about all evening and nothing mattered but the hardness of his body and the sureness of his lips, exploring her mouth with such persuasive excitement. Abandoned to their promise, Daisy murmured low in protest as Seth lifted his head at last and her arms clung to him instinctively until she opened her eyes and saw his smile.

Reality slammed back into place, and she snatched her hands away from him as if she had been stung. 'I...I have to go,' she muttered, backing dazedly away towards the taxi.

Seth stepped round her to hold the door open mockingly. 'Goodnight, Daisy Deare,' he said. 'Don't forget to bring your toothbursh tomorrow. From then on you'll be staying with me.'

'No, not that one.' Seth lowered his mobile phone irritably and pointed at another dress on the rack. 'Try the yellow,' he ordered before going back to his conversation.

Tight-lipped, Daisy stalked back to the changing-room. It was hard to believe that she had spent the entire night trying to deny the deep, treacherous desire that racked her whenever she thought about his kisses. Desire was the last thing on her mind now!

Seth had been thoroughly unpleasant ever since she had arrived that morning, very much on her dignity. Dictating orders to the ever-discreet Maria, he had barely acknowledged her arrival—merely jerking his head towards one of the bedrooms. 'You can put your things in there,' he had said by way of greeting, and had gone back to his dictation without another word. Then he had had the nerve to stride into the room and demand to see the clothes she had brought with her, proceeding to pour scorn over everything.

'You can leave that lot in the bag,' he said. 'I'm going to buy you a whole new wardrobe before I'm seen out in public with you.'

So here they were in this intimidatingly expensive shop with its even more intimidatingly expensive sales assistants, who kept producing outfits for Daisy to try on. Seth was carrying on some complex business negotiations over the phone, but he would break off when she appeared and either nod brusque approval of the outfit, in which case the assistants would add it to the growing collection on the rack, or reject it with some crushing comment before going back to his conversation. Daisy felt like one of the plastic dummies in the window, being pushed and pulled into position without a thought about what *she* wanted, and her blue eyes were bright with the effort of keeping a clamp on her fizzling temper.

Seth might at least show some interest. It was his idea for her to parade up and down like a walking coat-hanger, after all, but he spared only the most cursory glances at her between snarling orders down the phone. The person at the other end probably wasn't enjoying the situation any more than she was, thought Daisy, climbing bad-temperedly into the yellow dress. It served them both right for having anything to do with anyone as callous and unscrupulous and downright rude as Seth Carrington!

By the time Seth had snapped off his phone and decreed that she had enough clothes to be going on with the assistants were rubbing their hands at the thought of the final bill and Daisy was stiff with humiliation and resentment. He could hardly have made it clearer how unimportant she was, and the memory of last night's strumming awareness only made her crosser. If it hadn't affected Seth she certainly wasn't going to let him think that she had given it as much as a moment's thought!

Outside, the limousine was waiting arrogantly on the double yellow lines. Typical of Seth, Daisy decided furiously. He wouldn't care how many rules he broke to have his own way! George was helping the assistants load the bags into the back of the car while Seth stood by, wearing his saturnine expression. He glanced at his watch. 'Come on, we'll have to get back to the hotel. I've got a meeting in twenty minutes.'

'I'm going to walk,' said Daisy, looking stubborn, and he frowned irritably.

'What do you mean, walk?'

'Oh, haven't you ever tried it? It's quite easy when you get used to it. All you have to do is put one foot in front of the other.'

Seth's mouth tightened. 'Don't push me, Daisy. I'm not in the mood for it.'

'And I wasn't in the mood for being poked and prodded and looked over like some cow at market!' she snapped. 'Which is why I'm going to walk back to the hotel.'

Seth shot a warning look at George, who was holding open the car door with a wooden expression. 'I'm not going to argue with you in public,' he said, lowering his voice and turning slightly so that the chauffeur would not be able to hear. 'Do I have to remind you that we came to an agreement? You're here to do a job so stop acting like a spoilt brat and get in the car.'

Daisy had had enough. Her smile was right and dangerous as she stood on tiptoe and leant forward as if to kiss him on the cheek. With her lips close to his ear, she told him in unladylike terms exactly what he could do with his agreement. 'I'll see you back at the hotel, *darling*,' she added sweetly, stepping back and deciding to make her getaway while the blank look of disbelief was still on Seth's face. She waggled her fingers at him in a last provocative gesture. 'Bye-ee!' She turned and swung away along the street, her eyes still bright with temper but buoyed up with exhilaration at having got the better of Seth in this encounter at least.

He wouldn't risk a scene in public, she was sure, but he would be very angry when she got back to the hotel. Too bad, thought Daisy defiantly. It wouldn't do any

harm for Seth to learn that he couldn't push her around
like he did everyone else!

Even so, it was with some relief that she risked a
glance behind her and saw the car sliding off in the other
direction. 'My round, I think, Mr Carrington!' she murmured to herself with satisfaction, but it wasn't all that
long before she began to wonder just how smart she had
been to set off without any money or even a jacket. The
sun had been shining when they'd left the hotel and Seth
had said that she wouldn't need her shabby old handbag,
but now, ominously, black clouds were blotting out the
sunshine. A gust of wind made Daisy shiver in her
sleeveless shirt and she rubbed her arms. Increasing her
pace, she headed up the street until a crack of thunder
announced a downpour and she began to run.

For a while she took refuge in a department store but
the air-conditioning on her wet skin only made her feel
colder, and when the rain showed no sign of letting up
she decided that there was nothing for it but to get back
to the hotel as fast as she could. It took her nearly an
hour. She was sodden and her feet were very sore by
the time she trailed into the lobby and leant wearily
against the lift button. Her hair was hanging in rat's tails
and there were raindrops on the ends of her lashes, but
Daisy ignored the curious looks she was getting. All she
wanted now was to take off these clothes and put her
feet up.

Seth was in the middle of a meeting when she reached
the penthouse suite at last, and his guests looked up in
surprise at the bedraggled figure who practically fell
through the door. 'Back already, Daisy?' Seth's voice
was smooth but his eyes promised revenge. 'Did you
enjoy your walk?'

'Very refreshing,' said Daisy with a defiant look,

rather spoiling the effect by hobbling off to her room
where she collapsed onto the bed.

She had recovered enough to peel off her wet clothes
and was rubbing her hair with a towel when Seth came
in. She had heard his guests leaving and was trying not
to feel nervous about the inevitable showdown.

'I hope you've walked off your bad temper,' he said
in a cutting voice. Framed in the doorway, he was a
massive, intimidating presence and Daisy wished that
her heart wouldn't lurch so uncomfortably whenever he
appeared. 'You needn't think you can get away with
behaving like a sulky child tonight.'

Daisy had had enough time to regret her show of defiance which, in retrospect, *did* seem a bit childish, but
Seth's attitude only made her temper flare again. 'It
might help if *you* didn't behave like an arrogant, obnoxious *pig*!' she snapped back, towelling her hair so vig-
orously that it stood up on end.

'Is that all the thanks I get for providing you with an
entire new wardrobe?' he asked sardonically.

'I was perfectly happy with my old one,' retorted
Daisy. 'I'd much rather look *cheap*, as you call it, than
go through that again. If you'd wanted a dummy that
you could dress up and train to bleat "Yes, Seth; No,
Seth; You're absolutely marvellous, Seth" whenever
you pulled its string, you should have pinched one from
a shop window!'

'It would certainly have been a lot easier on my temper,' said Seth, a muscle jumping warningly in his jaw.

Daisy was still looking mutinous, oblivious to the
ridiculous contrast between her cross expression and the
wildly tousled hair as she tossed the towel aside. 'I'm
amazed you ever made any money, jackbooting all over
everybody the way you do,' she grumbled. 'Haven't you

ever heard of management skills and getting the best out of your employees by treating them like human beings?'

'I don't need any lessons from you on how to treat my employees,' he said, tight-lipped. 'I've never had any complaints about staff relations.'

'That's probably because they're all too terrified to say anything!'

Seth was completely exasperated by now. 'In that case, it's a pity *you're* not more terrified. I might get some peace, then!'

'I'm not scared of you,' said Daisy, tilting her chin in a characteristic gesture. 'I'm just fed up with being treated like a tiresome child instead of a grown woman.'

'Well, you know the answer to that, don't you, Daisy?' Reaching the doorhandle, Seth prepared to shut her in with her sulk. 'If you want to be treated like a woman, you'd better start behaving like one.'

CHAPTER FOUR

DETERMINED to prove to Seth that she wasn't the adolescent he so clearly thought her, Daisy spent the entire afternoon in the hotel's luxurious beauty salon—culminating in a make-over that so transformed her that she was taken aback by her own reflection when the beautician finally stood back.

She had subtly enhanced Daisy's fine bone structure and the blue eyes looked dark and almost witchy, although the sultry effect was rather spoiled by the irrepressibly tilting corners of her wide mouth which continued to look as if it were smiling no matter how hard Daisy sucked in her cheeks and pouted at the mirror.

Still, she *did* look more sophisticated, Daisy decided—rather pleased with her reflection. The hairdresser had trimmed her curls and scrunched them up between her fingers as she dried them so that although they were still hopelessly tousled they somehow looked as if she meant them to be that way, rather than looking as if she had simply forgotten to comb them. It made all the difference.

Seth hadn't even bothered to ask where she was going when she stalked out of the suite, merely ordering her over his shoulder to be ready to go out to a reception at seven o'clock. Daisy was rather hoping to stun him with her transformation when she went back in but, as it was, he didn't even glance up from the phone. There was obviously some kind of meeting going on. Several other men were grouped around on the chairs, all looking def-

erential and waiting obsequiously for Seth to finish his
conversation.

He was ignoring them, of course, bandying million-
dollar figures around with that arrogant assurance that
set Daisy's teeth on edge. She regarded him with hostile
eyes for a few seconds and then, when it was obvious
that her entrance had not even been noticed, stomped off
to her room and slammed the door shut.

Later, she could hear the murmur of sycophantic
goodbyes. Probably all bowing as they backed out of the
door, thought Daisy sourly. No wonder Seth was so arrogant if they let him trample over everyone like that!
She waited for him to come barging into her room. After
two minutes alone he must get withdrawal symptoms
from not having anyone to bully, but—frustratingly—he
didn't give her the opportunity of reminding him that
she at least was capable of standing up to him or of
knocking him sideways with her new-found sophistication. Instead, he knocked at the door and called out to
her that they would be leaving in half an hour.

'Come out when you're ready,' he added—without
sounding as if he particularly cared whether she did or
not—and then strolled off, leaving Daisy crosser than
ever.

She dressed sulkily in one of the outfits which Seth
had picked out for her, a stunningly simple sleeveless
yellow dress with a scoop neck and chunky ethnic bracelets racked up her arms. Exactly thirty minutes later she
jerked open her door and stalked out, to find Seth sitting
on the edge of one of the sofas and frowning down at
some papers spread out on the coffee-table.

Having spent the whole day in a state of simmering
temper, Daisy was torn between longing to tell Seth exactly what she thought of him and an equally burning
desire to prove to him that she could be just as feminine

and alluring as Astra Bentingger—if only he would acknowledge her existence for long enough. The indecision found expression as truculence and the blue eyes
held a mixture of hostility and challenge that sat oddly
with the sophisticated make-up and the artful simplicity
of the dress.

Seth looked up from the coffee-table and an arrested
expression came into his eyes as he took in Daisy's
tense, slender figure. The yellow suited her perfectly and
with her carefully tousled hair, clever make-up and com-
bative expression she looked both startlingly vivid and
unexpectedly beautiful.

Dropping some papers onto the table, Seth got slowly
to his feet. 'Well, well!' he said appreciatively, and came
across to where Daisy still stood defiantly outside her
door. He was wearing a beautifully cut grey suit with a
pale silk tie that made him look intimidatingly suave.
When he wasn't frowning or being unbearably arrogant
he was a disturbingly attractive man, and Daisy felt the
belligerence trickle away to leave her with an odd, empty
sensation that made her suddenly uncertain. She scowled
harder to disguise it as Seth came to stand in front of
her.

'Are you satisfied now that I'm not a schoolgirl?' Her
voice wasn't quite as steady as she would have liked.

His cool gaze assessed her lazily. 'It's certainly a great
improvement,' he admitted, and a smile just touched the
corners of his mouth. 'But you still don't look quite
right...'

Daisy heaved an exaggerated sigh. 'What's the matter
with me *now*?'

Seth took her wrist and ran his hands almost thoughtfully over the chunky bracelets and up her arms to her
shoulders. 'There's just something about your expression,' he explained.

'What's wrong with it?' What was it about his touch that melted her bones? Horribly aware of his nearness— of his hands on her bare skin—Daisy concentrated on stiffening her knees and avoiding Seth's eyes.

'You don't look much like a woman going out to spend an evening with her lover, do you?'

'Don't worry, I'll start smiling as soon as we walk out the door,' she said to his shoulder. 'There isn't much point in me standing here with a stupid smile pinned to my face, is there?'

She was trying not to quiver as Seth's thumbs caressed the soft skin of her inner arms. 'I don't want you smiling,' he said softly.

'What *do* you want, then?' Her attempt to sound tart didn't quite come off.

'I want you to look as if we've just rolled out of bed and can't wait to get back.'

The colour rose in Daisy's cheeks. 'How am I supposed to look like that?'

His hands smoothed along her shoulders and up her throat. 'You could use some of your supposed acting skills,' he suggested. 'I haven't seen much evidence of *them* yet.'

'I'll start acting as soon as we've got an audience,' she said, breathless beneath the searing touch of the fingers that were drifting beneath her curls.

'Or,' Seth went on as if she hadn't spoken, 'I could give you some intensive direction…like this,' he finished as his mouth came down on hers and Daisy's resistance was swamped in a wave of thrilling, treacherous pleasure.

His lips were so warm, so persuasive, so *right*. She struggled against the sensation but nothing could stop the instinctive clutch of desire or the electric excitement which ran like a current between them, cancelling out anger and antagonism and kindling something deep and delightful and infinitely more dangerous.

Seth's hands were cupping the back of her head, tangling in her curls and toppling her towards him so that Daisy really had no choice but to cling to him. Before she quite knew how it happened her arms were encircling him beneath his jacket, feeling the flex of steely muscles below his shirt. His arrogance, his ruthlessness, her own desperate defiance...all counted for nothing when Seth's mouth possessed hers with such tantalising warmth and Seth's hands were sliding lingeringly over her body and Seth's body was solid and unyielding against hers. The only thing that counted was the spinning excitement and the odd, inexplicable sense that as long as his arms were around her she was utterly and completely safe.

They yellow dress was rucked up where Seth was exploring the warm, silken length of her thigh with growing insistence, and Daisy murmured low in her throat as his lips travelled slowly, seductively around to her ear to nibble the tender lobe. 'Is that any clearer, Daisy Deare?'

His words filtered slowly through to Daisy's reeling mind. Hazy with pleasure and disorientated by the pounding, pulsing excitement, she could only blink dazedly at Seth as he put her away from him.

'Clearer?'

He let go of her shoulders, not without reluctance. 'I was trying to show you how to look like a woman in love, but I don't think you really need much direction from me. You're doing it perfectly now.'

Daisy opened her mouth to speak, found she couldn't frame a single intelligible word and shut it again. Her eyes were the colour of a summer night, huge and dark

and vulnerable in her pale face. She swallowed.
'H-hadn't we better go?' she managed to croak at last.

'I think you'd better put on some more lipstick first.'

Her hands were shaking so much that she had to hold
one still with the other before she could control the lipstick anywhere near her mouth. She was burning with
humiliation and resentment at the pathetic way she just
melted into Seth whenever he touched her, but far, far
worse was the smouldering, unsatisfied desire. She hated
the way that Seth could coolly stand there and behave
as if he knew nothing about the wild rush of excitement
that had swept all before it. She hated herself for wishing
that he would come into the bathroom and pull her back
into his arms and let reality sink, unnoticed and unre-
gretted, beneath the wave of passion once more.

For Daisy, the reception was a blur. She discovered
later that it had been held in aid of a well-known charity
but at the time there seemed something surreal about
seeing so many famous people crushed together, all talking at the tops of their voices. For some reason the reception was being held in an equally famous jeweller's
and they had to circulate among glass cases, containing
fabulous displays of jewellery. Daisy stared down at
them and tried not to think about Seth's hand touching
her elbow or resting possessively at her waist.

He was a much better actor than she was. As soon as
they got out of the car Daisy had pinned a bright smile
onto her face, but she was sure it must look as forced
as it felt and all her movements were stiff and jerky.

Seth, on the other hand, was relaxed, smiling, utterly
assured. He wasn't acting, she had to remind herself.
This was just the other side of Seth Carrington. She had
seen only the ruthless power of a tycoon but it was clear
that everyone here saw Seth very differently. For them

he was one of the crowd—someone who would cross the Atlantic for a party without even thinking about it.

Watching him, Daisy tried to see him through their eyes—rich, charming and imbued with that elusive, indefinable glamour—but it didn't work. They saw the jet-setter—she saw only the man whose touch turned her bones to molten honey.

The man whose hands had been warm and sure against her skin.

The man she would be alone with tonight.

Daisy gulped down the last of her champagne and gratefully allowed her glass to be refilled. She really must pull herself together. How many times did she have to tell herself that this was just a play in which she had little more than a walk-on part? and if she didn't make more of an effort she would lose even that. Seth might look urbane and charming this evening, but she had good reason to know just how heartless and objectionable he really was.

Another glass of champagne bolstered her confidence. She could see the covert glances people were giving her, wondering how anyone so unlikely had managed to ensnare Seth Carrington.

'How did you two meet?' asked a woman Seth had introduced simply as Frances, not bothering to disguise her surprise. She had streaky blonde hair brushed away from her face, a voice that set Daisy's teeth on edge and the same air of glossy self-assurance as everyone else in the room. She had also kissed Seth with what Daisy considered to be quite unnecessary warmth.

'Seth interviewed me for a job,' said Daisy before he could speak. Her smile was brilliant as she leant winsomely against him. 'It was love at first sight, wasn't it, darling?'

His hand tightened fractionally against her. 'It was for

me,' he agreed, and Daisy was delighted to see that Frances looked very put out.

'You *are* honoured,' she said to Daisy with an unbecoming titter. 'Seth's been through so many girls we all lost count years ago, but he was always a real brute and refused to say that he loved any of them.' She glanced accusingly at Seth and it was obvious that she had been one herself. 'You used to claim that love wasn't a word in your vocabulary!'

'I've only learnt it since I met Daisy,' he said, and drew her closer to underline the point.

For a brief moment Daisy allowed herself to relax into him and imagine that it was all true. His arm was steady around her and there was something immensely comforting about the solid strength of his body. What would it be like if he was holding her because he loved her, and not because he was trying to preserve the secrecy of his pre-nuptial contract with Astra Bentingger?

The thought of Astra was enough to make Daisy draw herself away on the excuse of having her glass topped up by a passing waiter. She felt as if her body was imprinted with the outline of Seth's arm, and she couldn't look at him. The sight of James Gifford-Gould pushing his way through the throng towards them was a welcome distraction. Relieved, Daisy greeted him with an enthusiasm that made Seth stiffen.

James's blue bedroom eyes roamed over her appreciatively and he insisted on kissing her as if they had been friends for a lifetime. 'You look delicious,' he told Daisy. 'Quite good enough to eat!'

'Where's Eva?' asked Seth pointedly.

'With her husband, I should imagine,' said James carelessly. 'I'm not very popular, anyway, after spending all last night speculating about *you*,' he added to Daisy. 'Eva said I was positively boring.'

All the champagne was beginning to have a euphoric effect on Daisy, who hadn't had any lunch. This was her opportunity to show Seth that some men were prepared to treat her like a woman! Buoyed up by alcohol and James's admiration, she proceeded to flirt outrageously with him—making great play with her eyelashes and checking Seth's reaction out of the corner of her eye. A muscle was beginning to beat satisfactorily in his cheek, she noted, quite exhilarated by her own hitherto unsuspected ability to dazzle.

It wasn't long before he dragged her forcibly away from James, but Daisy was well away by then and in no time at all had acquired a whole circle of admiring men. Seth had obviously decided to appear indulgent, but his eyes held a distinct warning which she deliberately ignored. He had either ignored her or been unpleasant to her all day, so it was just too bad if he didn't like her being the centre of attention for a change!

She had reached the giggly stage by the time they moved on to a restaurant for dinner with several others, including James who had managed to attach himself to the group. 'For God's sake, stop making a fool of yourself!' Seth hissed in her ear as they sat down, but that only set Daisy off into another fit of giggles. By the time she had recovered from that, James had won a good-natured argument over who was to sit on her other side and was intent on monopolising her again.

Seth's carefully indulgent look was beginning to look rather frayed by the end of the meal. Daisy was very conscious of his simmering irritation beside her, but as the food sobered her up slightly the thought of being alone with him was enough to make her stupidly nervous again and her flirting began to take on a more desperate quality.

When James suggested going on to a club after the

meal she seized on the idea. 'Yes, let's!' she cried. 'I
love dancing!'

The club was dark and crowded and pounding with
music. Daisy danced with James, but was enraged to see
Seth take another girl by the hand and pull her onto the
dance floor. Giving James the benefit of her most dazzling smile, she moved invitingly closer.

'You're so sweet, Daisy,' he said. 'Seth's much too
much of a bastard for you. Why don't you come home
with me instead?' he murmured close to her ear.

'Hmm?' she said absently, manoeuvring to keep Seth
and his partner in eyesight.

Taking the lack of a definite no as encouragement,
James spent the rest of the number trying to persuade
her to leave Seth. Daisy couldn't believe that their light-
hearted flirtation had suddenly turned into something serious, but she was uncomfortably aware that she *had*
encouraged him so she couldn't be too rude. She tried
to wriggle unobtrusively away but his arms only got
tighter and tighter, and it was an enormous relief to see
Seth suddenly appear beside them.

'I think it's time I took my lady away,' he said. There
was a grim look about his mouth, and James found himself hastily releasing Daisy. Muttering something in-
audible, he disappeared through the dancers and left Seth
to take Daisy into his arms. From a distance it must have
looked as if he couldn't wait to hold her, but his voice
was glacial in her ear.

'We'll have this one dance and then we're going,' he
said. 'So you'd better make it look good.'

Daisy suddenly realised that she was very tired and
had a terrible headache. In the circumstances, even the
lash of Seth's tongue couldn't make his arms seem less
than wonderfully inviting. With a tiny sigh she gave in
to temptation and leant into him, sliding her arms around

his neck and resting her face against his throat. They were hardly moving. Seth laid his cheek against her hair and held her close, and the tension which had kept Daisy sparkling all evening seeped slowly away.

She was practically asleep when Seth put her from him. 'That ought to do,' he said callously and, taking her by the wrist, he pulled her towards the entrance. 'I trust they're all thinking that we can't wait to get home to bed so they won't be surprised if you don't make your farewells.'

Outside the freshness of the night air made Daisy's head reel, and she was glad to fall into the waiting limousine. On the other hand, walking might have woken her up. Her head kept nodding onto Seth's rigid shoulder, only to be pushed firmly away by the flat of his hand. He was very angry about something, Daisy realised blearily, but she didn't realise just how angry he was until he propelled her roughly out of the lift and into the suite, shutting the door behind them with a snap that penetrated even Daisy's befuddled brain. Suddenly she was much more awake than she wanted to be.

Striding over to the table, Seth pulled out a cheque-book and flipped it open. 'How much is twenty-four hours of your time worth?' he asked in a harsh voice.

Daisy might be awake but she still wasn't quite steady, and had to cling to the back of one of the dining-chairs for support. 'Worth?' she echoed blankly. 'What do you mean?'

'I mean that I'm calling an end to this charade,' said Seth and she stared at him, appalled.

'You can't do that!'

'Oh, yes, I can,' he said grimly. 'And you can think yourself lucky that I'm prepared to pay you at all after the exhibition you made of yourself this evening! You're supposed to be an actress, for God's sake. If getting drunk and wrapping yourself around James Gifford-Gould was the best you could do I'm not surprised that you never get offered any decent parts.'

Daisy winced at his tone. 'I was just nervous,' she tried to excuse herself, but Seth only gave an incredulous laugh.

'Nervous?' he said. '*Nervous*? I've never seen anything less nervous than the way you carried on with James tonight! I practically had to prise you apart!'

'I thought you'd want me to be pleasant to your friends,' she said in a small voice.

'If you thought I'd want you to spend the entire evening crawling over another man you must be even more stupid than you look,' said Seth blisteringly, and Daisy quailed.

'I—I didn't, she stammered, but, to tell the truth, her memory was rather hazy already. Why, why, why had she drunk so much champagne?

'I knew you were wrong right from the start,' he continued savagely, as if she hadn't spoken. 'You don't look right, you don't dress right and you've absolutely no idea how to behave.'

'But what about our agreement?' stammered Daisy, stone cold sober by now.

'Since you haven't stuck by a word of it I hardly think you're in a position to quote it back at me now,' he pointed out with a cold look. 'All I asked was that you did as you were told but you couldn't even manage that, could you? You've been nothing but trouble, and I'm not putting up with you any longer.'

Daisy was still clutching the back of the chair. 'But you've told everyone that you're in love with me now,' she said desperately. 'What are they all going to think when I disappear?'

Seth shrugged. 'I'll tell them that you turned out to

be a little tramp, like all the others,' he said with callous indifference. 'It would be the truth, after all, and no one who saw you tonight with James would have any difficulty in believing it.'

'What about Astra?' Daisy was clutching at straws and it showed in her voice. 'If you get rid of me you won't have a decoy any longer.'

'I'll find someone else,' said Seth flatly. 'And next time I'll make sure I get a girl who doesn't argue!' He scribbled out the cheque and tossed it contemptuously across the table towards Daisy. 'Here. Consider yourself paid off.' Closing the cheque-book, he dropped it onto the polished table where it landed with a slap. 'You can stay here tonight,' he said, as if regretting even that concession, 'but I want you out in the morning.'

What had she done? Aghast at her sudden change of fortune, Daisy saw her only chance of finding Tom dissolving like mist in the morning. She couldn't let it go now! Swallowing, she levered herself away from the chair and faced Seth squarely.

'No,' she said.

Seth stared at her as if he had never heard the word before. He probably didn't hear it that often, Daisy thought irrelevantly. 'What do you mean, "*no*"?' he asked in a dangerously quiet voice.

Steeling herself, she held her ground. 'I'm not leaving in the morning. We had a deal.'

'Which you invalidated by doing the exact opposite of what you agreed.' Seth's expression was implacable.

'I convinced people that I was your girlfriend,' said Daisy stubbornly. 'That was all you asked me to do, and I did it.'

'If anyone really thought you and I were a couple they'd have changed their minds by the end of the evening,' said Seth in a harsh voice. 'What else do you think they would have made of the way you were flirting with James Gifford-Gould?'

'They probably just thought that I was trying to make you jealous because you weren't paying me any attention.'

'I was beside you all evening,' he was stung into objecting.

'Yes, but it was obvious that you weren't interested in *me*,' said Daisy bravely. 'As far as you were concerned, I was a rather tiresome necessity that you had to drag around with you—and it showed. Any other girl would have flirted with James in exactly the same way if you'd treated her the way you treated me all evening.'

Seth opened his mouth to retort, then shut it again with a snap. 'I'm not going to get into an argument,' he said tightly after a moment. 'The deal's off. You're leaving tomorrow, and that's that.'

Daisy clutched her hands together. 'If you make me leave I'll go straight to James Gifford-Gould and tell him everything about you and Astra,' she said, amazed at how steady her voice sounded. 'If he's the gossip you say he is it'll be in all the papers before you have time to set up another girl as a diversion.'

There was a long, blistering silence. Seth didn't move, but his very stillness was terrifying and the expression in his eyes made Daisy's heart contract nervously.

'That's blackmail,' he said at last, very softly.

'I...I know.'

'Blackmail's a very dangerous game,' Seth went on in the same unnervingly quiet voice. 'A very dangerous game indeed.'

Daisy bit her lip. 'I just want to stick to our original agreement so that I can go to the Caribbean with you. I'll really make an effort from now on, I promise, and I won't argue.' She glanced at Seth's face but his expression was impossible to read. 'Even if people did suspect that there was something wrong tonight we could always say that we had a row and then made it up,' she went on with a tinge of desperation. 'Please?'

'Blackmailers don't usually say please,' said Seth caustically. 'I don't believe you'd do it, anyway.'

'I would,' said Daisy quickly, mentally kicking herself. Lifting her chin, she met Seth's hard grey gaze with a boldness she was far from feeling. 'Try me!'

The atmosphere was taut with tension as they faced each other across the table. Daisy's legs were trembling, but she kept her head high and hoped that her nervousness didn't show. She hated the very idea of blackmail, but if she wanted to find Tom for Jim she would just have to live with it.

It was Seth who broke the silence first. Walking round the table, he took Daisy's stubborn chin in an ungentle hand. 'All right,' he said, his fingers digging into her soft skin, 'we'll compromise. You can have tomorrow to prove that you can behave like a real girlfriend. If you can last the day without arguing or sulking or coming on to other men you can stay. But one lapse and you're out, blackmail or no blackmail. Is that understood?'

Daisy nodded, and to her relief he released her chin. Gingerly she rubbed her face where he had gripped her.

Seth's voice was as implacable as his eyes. 'You might have got away with it this time, but if you cross me again, Daisy, I can promise you that you'll regret it. So if you're wise you'll keep your hands off other men. If there's any flirting to be done it had better be with *me*!'

Daisy woke up with a dry mouth, a thumping headache and a sick sense of disaster which got worse as snatches of the previous night came back to her. She remembered staring down at a diamond and sapphire necklace and being hideously aware of Seth's arm around her waist. They had gone to some restaurant after that, hadn't they? Daisy had no idea how they had got there or what she had eaten, but she had a nasty feeling that she had laughed too much.

Oh, God, had she made a terrible fool of herself? The rest of the night was a blur. She had a confused memory of dancing with James and of the hard reassurance of Seth's body...but if they had been dancing why did she think that he had been angry? She had a vivid picture of contemptuous grey eyes and the lash in his voice, and the thump in her head became deafening.

What had she done?

She felt marginally more civilised after a shower, but the hangover was still throbbing along every nerve and everything about her seemed to be out of focus. Still, Seth would have to be faced some time. Incapable of making a decision about what to wear, Daisy wrapped herself in a white towelling robe and opened the bedroom door gingerly.

Seth was fully dressed and looked painfully awake. He was sitting at the table, drinking coffee and reading the *Financial Times* but at the sound of the door he lowered the newspaper and regarded Daisy over the top. Her hair was still damp from the shower and, without last night's make-up, she looked pale and fragile and much younger as she hung onto the door and clutched her head.

'Do you want some breakfast?'

Daisy blenched at the very idea. She tried to shake her head, but it hurt too much and she gave up. 'I just want to die,' she muttered honestly, and reluctantly amusement lit Seth's hard grey eyes.

'You'll feel better if you have something. What about some coffee?'

'I might manage some tea,' said Daisy, creeping over to the table like an old woman as Seth ordered over the phone. She sat down very carefully and propped her head in her hands. 'What happened last night?'

'Don't you remember?'

'Only bits.'

Seth poured himself some coffee. 'You behaved appallingly,' he told her, and Daisy gave a groan that turned into a moan as her head threatened to split open.

'What did I do?'

'Just about everything that you weren't supposed to do,' said Seth, but it was almost as if he was having to make an effort to sound severe. 'You ignored me completely, flirted outrageously with every other man you came across, made a complete and utter exhibition of yourself over James Gifford-Gould and finished off the evening with a spot of blackmail.'

'Blackmail?' echoed Daisy, aghast.

'I was threatening to throw you out, and you said that if I did you'd make sure everyone knew the truth about our deal.'

Oh, God, it was all coming back! 'I'm t-terribly sorry,' she stammered. 'I don't know what came over me.'

'Too many bottles of champagne, I should think,' said Seth with a touch of his old acidity.

There was a knock at the door, and a waiter brought in Daisy's tea. Seth waited until he had gone before he turned back to Daisy, who was pouring herself a cup with a distinctly unsteady hand. 'Do I gather that blackmail wasn't part of a well-thought-out plan on your part?'

'Of course not!' said Daisy, horrified.

'You were very convincing,' he pointed out.

'I just didn't want to lose the job,' she muttered, spooning sugar into her tea and stirring carefully to avoid the chink of silver against china.

Seth studied the damp, dark head bent over her tea, a slight frown between his brows. 'You certainly tried hard enough to lose it last night.'

Daisy looked up at that. Her eyes looked enormous in her white face. 'D-do you want me to go?'

There was a tiny pause. 'We reached a compromise,' he said after a moment, and there was a note in his voice that Daisy couldn't place. 'You've got today to prove to me that you're worth keeping after all.'

Her shoulders slumped in relief. 'Thank you!'

'But you'd better behave,' Seth warned her, as if regretting the concession already.

'Oh, I will,' she promised fervently. 'No one will guess that I'm not completely besotted with you.'

Seth grunted and picked up his newspaper. 'You won't look very besotted with a hangover like that,' he said. 'You'd better go back to bed.'

CHAPTER FIVE

WAKING again a couple of hours later, Daisy blinked cautiously at the ceiling and decided that she felt better. The hangover still had her in its woolly grip, but her headache had subsided. At least she could sit up without feeling as if her head was about to fall off.

Had she really had the nerve to blackmail Seth? Daisy quailed at the thought. She was lucky that he hadn't thrown her out there and then! If she wanted to get to the Caribbean to find Tom she couldn't afford another lapse like that. From now on she would do exactly as Seth said, she promised herself as she dressed carefully in the narrow trousers, long, soft shirt and waistcoat that he had bought her yesterday. The effect managed to be casual and subtly expensive at the same time. She could do with being a bit more subtle herself, thought Daisy ruefully, and looked a little nervously at the door. It was time she proved to Seth once and for all that it was worth keeping her.

When she went out Seth was talking to a stout man with a round, jovial face, but they both got up to their feet at the sight of her. 'Feeling better?' asked Seth, carefully expressionless.

Remembering her resolve, Daisy took a deep breath and walked over to him. 'Much, thank you,' she said with a smile, and reached up to kiss him quite naturally on the cheek.

She felt Seth stiffen in surprise, and then his arm went around her to hold her at his side. 'This is Henry

Huntington, darling,' he said, and introduced her in her turn.

Henry had twinkling eyes that turned down at the corners. Daisy thought that he looked rather nice. 'Have you been ill?' he asked in concern.

'It's all self-inflicted,' said Daisy honestly. 'I'm paying the price for not listening to Seth last night!' Perhaps she should have pretended that she had been ill after all? Seth might think that it sounded too unsophisticated to have a girlfriend who suffered from hangovers, but when she glanced at him she saw with relief that although he was pretending to look disgusted he was grinning. His smile seemed to vibrate right through her, but she didn't move out of his arm.

Henry was sympathetic. He looked like a man who had suffered from plenty of hangovers in his time. 'We heard that Seth had turned up with a sparkling new girl,' he went on, beaming. 'Johnny was very taken with you! He said that it was wonderful to come across a girl who knew how to enjoy herself,' he added to Seth. 'You know what most of the girls at that sort of do are like— so busy looking right that they can't be bothered to actually talk to you. Johnny said that your Daisy was much more fun.'

'She wasn't much fun this morning,' said Seth drily, but his arm tightened around her.

'No, I'm afraid I'm in disgrace,' Daisy added, wondering who Johnny was and how she had managed to make such an impression on him.

Henry laughed. 'I shouldn't worry,' he told her comfortingly. 'You'll be able to bring him round. Nobody's ever seen Seth smitten before. I didn't believe it myself, but now that I've met you I can quite understand why. He's always been a bit of a cool customer, but everyone's talking about how he's met his match at last!'

'They are?' Too late, Daisy remembered that she wasn't supposed to sound so surprised but Henry didn't seem to notice anything odd.

'Yes, the word is that he didn't take his eyes off you all evening.'

'I was just waiting to catch her before she slid under the table,' said Seth, and they all laughed. Daisy's laugh wasn't quite as hearty as Henry's. She knew that Seth wasn't joking. He had met his match all right—but in Astra, not in her—and all last night proved was that he was a much better actor than she was.

'Were you talking business?' she asked after a moment. 'Am I interrupting?'

'Of course not,' said Henry gallantly, and Seth drew her down into an armchair.

'Henry and Elizabeth have asked us to stay this weekend,' he said, perching above her on the arm of the chair so that he could slide his fingers beneath her hair and stroke her neck. 'They've got a wonderful old place in Gloucestershire.'

'We'll be quite a party,' Henry added. 'There's a ball in aid of charity on the Saturday night, so Elizabeth is getting everyone organised for dinner beforehand. Should be rather fun. Do say you'll come.'

He looked at Daisy who glanced a little uncertainly at Seth. 'That sounds lovely,' she said, not sure whether she was supposed to be accepting or making an excuse. 'Are we doing anything this weekend?'

'Nothing we can't do just as well in the country,' said Seth smoothly. 'Thanks, Henry. We'd like to come.'

Henry stayed for another half-hour. Daisy did her best to live up to the sparkling reputation that the unknown Johnny had given her, but she was increasingly distracted by Seth's fingers massaging her neck. They were warm and strong and sent disturbing shivers of sensation

down her spine, but her headache had completely gone
and it was wonderfully comforting to lean against his
body where he sat on the arm of the chair. It was just
for Henry's benefit, Daisy tried to tell herself, but when
he rose to go she couldn't help feeling a stab of disappointment as Seth released her and got to his feet as well.

She was on her best behaviour all day. Maria arrived
soon after Henry had left, and she and Seth worked
through a huge pile of correspondence. 'Do you mind if
I make a phone call?' Daisy asked, feeling guilty at seeing them so busy.

'Of course not.' Seth looked at her almost suspiciously. 'You're very docile, Daisy—or are you still
hung-over?'

'I thought you wanted me docile?'

'Yes, but am I going to have to pour five bottles of
champagne down you every night to keep you that way?'

'I'm sticking to mineral water from now on,' said
Daisy with feeling, and he gave one of his sudden, unexpected smiles that so transformed the harsh face and
made her go weak at the knees.

'I'll believe that when I see it!'

Daisy escaped to her room and sank rather shakily
down onto the bed. She couldn't afford to go to pieces
whenever he smiled at her! That was how she had got
into so much trouble last night. She had to remember
that for Seth she was just an understudy, and that he
would be smiling at Astra long after she had fulfilled
her purpose and gone.

She rang her mother at the flower shop they ran together. 'Are you sure you're all right?' Ellen asked worriedly.

'I'm fine, Mum, honestly.'

'There was a picture of you in Lisa's paper,' her

mother went on. 'You looked so different I hardly recognised you! And that man, Seth Carrington, was looking at you as if he was absolutely besotted! Are you sure
he's not...taking advantage?'

Daisy had to smile at her mother's old-fashioned no-
tions. 'I've told you, Mum, he's not interested in me at
all.' Uncomfortably aware of a wistful note in her voice,
she added briskly, 'He just wants to divert attention
away from his relationship with Astra Bentingger. Last
night was just an act.'

'He must be a very good actor if that photograph is
anything to go by,' said her mother with unusual tartness.

'He is.' Daisy only just managed to suppress a sigh
in time. 'How's Jim?' she changed the subject hurriedly.

'Much better.' Ellen's voice softened. 'I worry about
you with this man, Daisy, but I have to admit that it's
done Jim the world of good to hear that you're going to
the Caribbean. Just knowing that you'll have a chance
to trace Tom has cheered him up no end.'

Daisy put the phone down, feeling much better herself. If Jim's condition had improved then this interlude
with Seth was going to be worthwhile. And it *was* just
an interlude, she reminded herself sternly. She had better
not get used to this luxury, or think too much about
Seth's smile or the feel of Seth's fingers on her neck.

Knowing that Jim was relying on her, Daisy was more
determined than ever not to jeopardise her chance of
getting to the Caribbean. She was so quiet that Seth kept
on glancing at her suspiciously, and was driven in the
end to ask her if she was all right.

'I'm fine,' said Daisy, dutifully leafing through a
magazine.

Seth frowned. 'I've invited a couple of people round
for drinks this evening but, if you're not feeling up to

it, I could cancel them.' The offer seemed to be wrenched out of him and Daisy had the feeling that it surprised him as much as her.

'Really, I'm fine.'

Seth's idea of a couple of people turned out to be at least ten. Daisy wore silk trousers and a matching sleeveless top with an embroidered mandarin collar. Seth might not have seemed to be concentrating when she was trying on all those different outfits, but it was clear that he had a much better idea of what would suit her than she did. Left to herself, she would never have chosen anything like this.

Mindful of her demure role, Daisy tried to keep her mouth shut and stick by Seth but people kept wanting to talk to her. It was evident that her sudden appearance as Seth's girlfriend had caused a good deal of talk but, to Daisy's surprise, no one seemed to doubt for a minute that they were a genuine couple. 'I'm not surprised Seth has fallen for someone like you at last,' an older woman called Victoria confided to her. 'He's always had some incredibly glamorous girl hanging on his arm, but it was obvious that he didn't care about any of them. You're different.'

'No one's ever described me as incredibly glamorous,' Daisy agreed a little sadly.

'No, but that's not what Seth needs. He's got plenty of glamour of his own. What he needs is someone warm and loving.' Victoria looked thoughtfully over at Seth, and then back to Daisy. 'Seth might have had a lot of lovers but I don't think he's ever had much loving. You could change all that.'

Stupidly, Daisy felt tears prick her eyes. What on earth was the matter with her? Astra Bentingger was probably just as good at loving as she was at everything else, and that was what Seth wanted. 'I'd like to try,' she said, but her words seemed to echo mockingly in her brain. She would never have the chance to love Seth as he needed to be loved, so there was no point in even thinking about it.

'This is just a performance,' she muttered to herself, and to prove it she put her hand deliberately through Seth's arm and rested her cheek against his shoulder. Just a performance.

It wasn't long before her jaw was rigid with smiling. As promised, she had stuck to mineral water but she was beginning to wonder if she should have had a drink after all—to keep her awake. Everyone else seemed to be settling down for a party, but all Daisy could think about was how little sleep she had had last night.

'What about dinner?' someone said what seemed like hours later. 'We could try that new place in Chelsea that everyone's talking about. What do you think, Seth?'

Seth glanced down at Daisy, who was sitting next to him on the sofa at that stage. She was smiling with great animation, but there was a drawn look around her dark blue eyes. 'Daisy's tired,' he said. 'I think we'll have a quiet night in.'

Judging by the looks of amazement the others were exchanging, Seth had never given any previous indication that he ever knew what a quiet night in *was*. The women were all looking at Daisy enviously and the men knowingly, and she shifted uncomfortably. 'I'm quite happy to go out,' she said, embarrassed.

'Don't say that,' said the man on her other side humorously. 'It's obvious Seth can't wait to get you to himself!'

At last they were all gone. Seth shut the door after them and turned back to Daisy. Having longed for everyone to go, she was suddenly acutely aware of the silence.

She cleared her throat. 'That seemed to go all right, didn't it?'

'Yes.' He sounded oddly preoccupied as he watched her and, for want of something to do, Daisy sat down again on the sofa.

'Didn't you want to go out to dinner? I thought the idea was that we were to go out and be seen together?'

'There's no need,' he told her. 'Everyone who was here tonight will go away and tell everyone else that I couldn't wait to get my hands on you. They're all assuming that we're in bed right now.'

Daisy felt a wave of heat wash over her and clamped down on the unnervingly vivid image of Seth undressing her; of him drawing her down onto the big bed and running his hands over her body. So clearly could she imagine it that she could almost swear that he was about to smile and hold out his arms and tell her that he hadn't been able to wait for everyone to go so that he could be alone with her.

But he didn't smile. He just stood there by the door, watching her with that odd expression on his face, while the air began to strum with an indefinable tension.

'What *are* we going to do?' Daisy asked, determined not to give in to it. 'Given that we're not, in fact, going to bed?' There, that was the right note—cool, unperturbed; the tone that said she wasn't in the least bit bothered about being alone with him.

There was a tiny pause and then Seth came down the steps into the sitting area. 'We could always have something to eat,' he said, picking up the phone and calling room service. 'There's no point in us starving just to convince everyone that we're in love.' His voice was as carefully impersonal as Daisy's had been.

An exquisite dinner was brought up to the suite and set out on the table before the waiters discreetly disappeared and left them alone again. Daisy had been keeping up a flow of brittle chatter to show Seth that being alone with him didn't affect her in the slightest, but it dried up as soon as they sat down at the table. There was something so intimate about sitting like this, with the room lit only by lamplight and two flickering candles on the table. Seth was near enough to touch. The candlelight threw a wavering light onto his face, softening the harsh lines, but his expression was impossible to read.

Daisy felt as if they were marooned together in stillness and silence, impossibly remote from the rest of London. She kept thinking that if there was anyone watching she could reach across the table to twine her fingers with his or lay her hand against his cheek...but there was no audience, and no need to pretend. That's all it would have been, she told herself fiercely—a pretence. She didn't really want to touch him. She didn't really want him to look up from his wine and smile.

A quivering had started somewhere deep inside her, vibrating through her until she felt as if all her edges were strumming. It must be tiredness that was making her react so strangely, Daisy thought desperately. Tiredness and the fact that she had spent most of the evening within the circle of Seth's arm and now, just when she had got used to it, it felt a bit odd without the steely solidity of his body to lean against.

At last the meal was over and the waiters came to clear the table, leaving coffee on the low table between the two sofas. Daisy didn't really want any, but she accepted a cup anyway. At least it would keep her hands occupied. Seth was lounging opposite her, with all the assurance and relaxed alertness of a big cat. It made Daisy nervous—the way he could sit there, simply drinking his coffee, and still fill the room with his presence.

She sat on the very edge of her chair, stirring her coffee needlessly. Was it her imagination, or could Seth feel the air twisting and tightening around them? Really, it was easier when they *were* pretending, she decided edgily.

'Well, I…I think I'll go to bed,' she said at last, and her cup rattled slightly in its saucer as she put it back onto the table.

Seth rose with her. 'Already?' he said. 'It's still early.'

'I didn't get much sleep last night.'

'No, you didn't, did you?' Seth's face was perfectly straight, but Daisy thought she could hear an undercurrent of amusement in his voice. Or was that just wishful thinking? 'This time last night you were only just beginning!'

Daisy took a deep breath. 'I'm sorry about last night,' she said hesitantly, 'but I've been all right today, haven't I?'

Seth looked down at her. In the shadowy light her eyes were dark and uncertain. 'You've been perfect,' he said slowly, as if realising it for the first time.

The quivery feeling inside her was getting worse. 'So we can stick to our original agreement?' she persevered, trying to keep her voice steadier than the rest of her.

'If that's what you want,' said Seth. He took her hands without haste and pulled her easily towards him. 'But we could always make one or two amendments.' His voice was deep and warm, and Daisy could feel it curling around her like a promise. 'What do you think?'

She stared up at him, torn by terrible temptation, knowing that all she had to do was smile and he would kiss her. Knowing that if he did she was lost. Already the desire that had been lurking all evening was seeping through her resistance and dissolving all her earlier resolutions about being cool and sensible and treating this like any other job.

Wavering, Daisy hesitated too long. The next moment the atmosphere was broken by the insistent ring of the telephone. Seth swore under his breath but released her hands to answer it, while Daisy stood where she had been left—unsure of whether she felt relieved or bitterly disappointed.

Seth picked up the receiver without ceremony. 'Yes?' he said, not even bothering to hide his irritation, but his tone changed abruptly when he heard who was on the line. 'Astra! I wasn't expecting you to call this evening.' There was a pause, and then he turned his back on Daisy and lowered his voice. 'Of course I'm glad to hear from you, honey,' he said.

Daisy didn't wait to hear any more. She went into her room and shut the door quietly but very deliberately so that he could not accuse her of eavesdropping on his conversation. The name Astra had been like a splash of cold water in her face.

How could she have forgotten Astra? Daisy sat on the edge of the bed and stared blankly at the wall. It was hard to believe that she had known Seth only two days. Already it seemed peculiarly natural to be with him. The atmosphere might be tense but she had never felt as if she didn't belong, even when he was being his most unpleasant.

And he wasn't always unpleasant... Daisy's blue eyes were dark and unfocused as she remembered the look in his eyes just before the phone rang. What would have happened if she hadn't hesitated? Would he have kissed her? Would he have let the phone ring and ring while he drew her into his room and down onto the wide bed?

Her heart clenched at the thought, and she stood up abruptly. She ought to be grateful that the phone had rung when it had. There was no point in getting involved with Seth Carrington. He was out of her league. He might take her to bed for a night or two—because she was there; because she was available—but that was all it would ever be. It was Astra he wanted, and she had better not forget it again.

If only she could forget what Victoria had said as well. 'What he needs is someone warm and loving.' Would Astra give Seth the loving he needed? Daisy thought of all that she had ever read about Astra Bentingger and somehow doubted it.

Well, it wasn't her problem, she told herself fiercely as she got ready for bed. She would have enough problems finding Tom and persuading him to come home and see Jim. Seth Carrington was more than capable of looking after himself, and he wouldn't thank her for doing anything stupid like falling in love with him.

Not that she *would* do anything stupid like that. Of course she wouldn't.

The next morning Daisy was determined to be pleasant but cool, and to impress on Seth that she hadn't even *thought* about kissing him last night. In the event, Seth was in such a bad mood that it obviously didn't matter how she behaved because nothing she did was going to be right, anyway. Having had her head bitten off three times for attempting to make polite conversation, Daisy gave up and subsided into a silence that was meant to be dignified but which was, in fact, rather sulky. What had made her think that she stood in any danger of falling in love with a man who was grumpy and disagreeable and altogether obnoxious? Astra Bentingger was welcome to him!

'Are you expecting any visitors today?' she asked frigidly as breakfast was cleared from the table.

Seth looked up, and the dark brows drew together in a suspicious frown. 'Why?'

'I was wondering if I was confined to quarters again or if I'd be allowed to go out, that's all.'

'You're not in gaol!' he snapped.

'It feels like it sometimes,' muttered Daisy and he scowled.

'As it happens, I've got business meetings all day and I'll be out to lunch as well. Where are you going?' he added abruptly. 'You weren't planning to sneak off and see Robert, were you?'

'Why should you care if I was?' she demanded sullenly.

Seth was gathering up papers and shoving them ferociously into a briefcase. 'Because someone might recognise you,' he said with exaggerated patience. 'I would have thought that was obvious!'

'No one you know is going to be in my part of town,' Daisy pointed out. She was hoping to visit Jim in hospital, but she didn't see any reason to tell Seth that in the mood he was in at the moment.

'So you *are* going to see him?'

'I might,' she said provocatively, and then regretted it as Seth swung round with a dangerous look on his face.

'I wouldn't advise it,' he said in a silky, terrifying voice. 'You might be surprised at the places I know people, and if I hear that you've been seen with another man I'll make you sorry that you ever tangled with me.'

'I'm sorry already!' grumbled Daisy without thinking.

Seth scowled. 'You were the one who was so keen to stay,' he reminded her bitingly. 'Or have you changed your mind now that you've recovered from your hangover?'

'No.' Daisy caught herself up. She mustn't let herself

get into an argument with him! 'I'm not going to see Robert, anyway. I…er…I just wanted to do some shopping.'

'Alone?'

She was tempted to point out that he was giving a pretty good impression of a gaoler for someone who was insisting that she wasn't in gaol, but wisely held her tongue and simply nodded.

Seth favoured her with a hard stare, as if not entirely convinced by her innocent look, but in the end he pulled a wad of money out of his briefcase and tossed it across to her. 'Here, you'd better take that.'

Daisy thought it safest not to argue. She had no intention of spending any of it, but at least it might convince him that she really was going shopping.

Jim was delighted to see her, and seemed to have no doubts that she would be able to trace Tom as soon as she arrived in the Caribbean. Daisy didn't have the heart to point out that it was unlikely to be as easy as that. He tired quickly so she kissed him and left after half an hour and made her way to the flower shop which she and her mother ran together. It was odd to be back among the buckets of lilies and roses and sweetly scented stocks.

Daisy had a real flair for floral arrangements and had built up a reputation for stunningly effective displays with that extra touch of class, but today she felt strangely removed from it all—in spite of the delighted welcome she received from her mother and their assistant, Lisa.

The shop was heady with the scent of the summer flowers, bright and beautiful in their buckets…so why did everything seem somehow colourless without Seth? She mustn't let this time with him spoil her for her real life, Daisy told herself sternly as she caught the bus back over the river to Knightsbridge. When this was over, and

she had found Tom, she would have to go back so there
was no point in getting used to a life of luxury.

There was no point in getting used to Seth.

At Knightsbridge she remembered that she was supposed to have been shopping, so she got off the bus and
bought herself a pair of flamboyant earrings in the shape
of fuschias to cheer herself up and to remind herself that
she was really a florist and not Seth Carrington's girlfriend at all.

It was another lovely hot afternoon, and she walked
slowly back to the hotel through the park. Everywhere
she looked there seemed to be couples lying on the grass,
absorbed in each other's company and oblivious to the
activity all around them. Daisy tried not to feel envious
or to imagine what it would be like if she and Seth were
an ordinary couple and could come and sit out here too,
just happy to be together.

Seth would never be ordinary, she accepted with an
inward sigh, and he wasn't likely ever to be happy with
her, so she might as well stop dreaming and get on with
what was, after all, just a job.

'Oh, so you've decided to come back, have you?' Seth
growled as soon as she let herself into the suite. He was
pacing the floor, tie loosened and shirtsleeves rolled up,
but in spite of the air-conditioning he looked hot and
cross, as if he was trying to disguise his relief at seeing
her.

'Well…yes,' said Daisy, surprised. 'I told you I was
going to be out. I didn't think you'd be back yet.'

'I came back early.' Seth stuck his hands in his pock-
ets and prowled around the back of the sofas. 'What
have you been doing all this time?' he asked abruptly.

'Oh, just wandering around,' she said airily.

'You don't seem to have done much shopping.'

Daisy produced her earrings. 'I bought these.'

'Is that *it*?' He stopped pacing for a moment to stare at her.

He was probably used to girls coming back laden with expensive bags and boxes, she realised belatedly. 'I couldn't really find anything I liked,' she said a little lamely, and dug in her bag for the money he had given her. 'Here's your money back. I didn't need it. Thank you, anyway,' she added politely.

That seemed to be the wrong thing to do, too. Hadn't anyone ever given him any money back before? Seth looked utterly taken aback for a moment before he recollected himself. 'Why don't you keep it?' he said in an odd voice. 'Spend it later.'

'I'd rather not,' said Daisy honestly. 'I don't feel comfortable carrying that amount of money around with me.'

There was a short silence. Why was he looking at her in that odd way? To ease the tension Daisy took out her pearl studs and hooked in the fuschia earrings, shaking her head so that they swung against her cheeks. 'What do you think?'

Seth didn't answer immediately. He watched the pink and purple flowers dangling on either side of Daisy's vivid face. 'Very you,' he said at last and then, abruptly, he smiled and the peculiar tension dissolved.

Daisy felt quite weak, although whether it was with relief or the effect of Seth's heart-clutching smile she wasn't sure. All she knew was that there was a warm sensation seeping along her veins and that the room suddenly seemed to be full of sunshine.

'Did your meeting finish earlier than you thought?' It was wonderful just to be able to ask an ordinary question without that edgy undercurrent in the air.

'It's still going on,' Seth admitted. He turned away and went over to stand by the window, looking out. 'I came back to find you. I wanted to apologise for snapping at you this morning. I was...preoccupied about something else.'

Daisy forced herself to ask. 'Something about Astra?'

'In a way. She rang again this afternoon while you were out. Apparently Dimitrios is acting very suspiciously, and she's told her lawyers to put a halt on the negotiations for the pre-nuptial contract for the time being.'

'Oh.' Daisy rolled the pearl studs in her palm and didn't look at Seth. 'Does...does that mean that you don't need me any more?' she asked tentatively, horrified at how her heart had plunged at the prospect.

'Far from it,' said Seth. 'If Dimitrios is suspicious then this is the very time to make sure that he and everybody else knows all about you.'

He didn't seem very upset at the way Astra had apparently put their relationship on hold, thought Daisy, but perhaps he considered her worth waiting for. Unaccountably depressed, she carried on fiddling with her earrings.

An odd, awkward silence fell. 'So...are we going out tonight?' Daisy broke it at last with an air of forced brightness.

Seth seemed to welcome the change of subject. The rigid tension relaxed from his shoulders and he turned from the window. 'We're invited out to dinner, but we don't have to be there until eight. What would you like to do until then?' He glanced at his watch. 'It's only a quarter to five now.'

'Don't you have work to do?' she said in surprise, and he shrugged.

'Nothing that can't wait.'

'But you don't have to entertain me,' said Daisy hesitantly.

'I know,' said Seth. 'Think of it as my way of making amends for being so unpleasant this morning.'

'Does that mean I have to make amends for being provoking?' she asked jokingly, unsure of how to react.

He looked at her with those unsettling grey eyes. 'Not unless you want to,' he said and, unfairly, he smiled.

Daisy's gaze skittered away from his. She had joined him at the window, and now she rested her hands on the sill and watched a young mother lean over a pushchair and give a toddler an ice-cream while Seth's smile burned in her mind. She was supposed to be being cool but polite. She was supposed to be keeping her distance. It would be much easier all round if she just went to her room and kept out of his way until they had to go out.

'Do you know what I'd really like to do?' she said slowly.

'What?'

'I'd like to go and have an ice-cream in the park.'

CHAPTER SIX

'YOU'RE very cheap to entertain, aren't you?' Seth was lounging on the grass, watching Daisy as she licked her ice-cream. His expression was indulgent, amused, but there was an odd undercurrent in his voice as he looked away across the Serpentine. 'A couple of hours with Astra is much more expensive.'

Daisy glanced at his averted profile, and then returned her attention to the ice-cream. 'It doesn't always cost much to enjoy yourself,' she said.

'That's not the impression you gave me when we first met,' Seth pointed out, and Daisy could feel the acute grey gaze resting on her once more. 'You told me then that you were only interested in money.'

'There's no denying that it helps sometimes,' she admitted with a sigh, thinking of the problems they had had ever since Jim had fallen ill. 'But needing money isn't the same as only being interested in it, and it doesn't mean that you can't ever be happy without it.' Finishing her ice-cream at last, she licked her fingers and looked about her thoughtfully. 'Things were very difficult for my mother after my father died, but she made sure that I still had a happy childhood. We didn't have a garden, and I used to love going to the park and feeding the ducks. Just having the space to run around was wonderful and sometimes on very special occasions, she would buy me an ice-cream and we'd sit on the grass, just like this.'

Daisy's dark blue eyes were soft with memory, but she smiled rather shamefacedly when she realised how dreary it must all sound to someone of Seth's back-ground. 'I suppose it must all seem rather boring, com-pared to what you were used to.'

He didn't answer immediately. 'Ice-cream's not very exciting when you can have it whenever you want,' he said at last. 'Nothing is. I had everything money could buy as a child, but I guess in the end my childhood was a lot less exciting than yours.'

'But you must have had so many opportunities!' pro-tested Daisy, sitting up. 'You must have seen so many wonderful places and done such wonderful things!'

'Oh, I used to get shunted around the world, yes.' Seth shrugged. 'My parents would pass me between them wherever they happened to be having their latest affair, but it didn't matter where they happened to be they al-ways lived in exactly the same way—shut away behind high walls with their own private beach and their own private swimming pool. If they went out it was only to visit friends who lived in exactly the same way.' His voice was threaded with bitterness. 'They might as well have stayed at home.'

'Couldn't *you* go out if you wanted to?'

'I was kidnapped when I was three,' said Seth as casu-ally as Daisy might have mentioned catching a bus. 'Af-ter that, they were all paranoid about security and I was never allowed outside the grounds on my own. Of course, as soon as I was old enough I rebelled and I used to run away regularly, but they would just send out a security firm to find me and take me back. I'd get beaten, but it was always worth it to get away for a while.' Leaning back on his hands, he watched two small boys who were playing with a model boat by the water's edge. 'My life might have seemed over-privileged to most peo-ple, but I used to envy kids whose only treat was a trip to the park occasionally.'

Daisy studied the dark face which was turned slightly away from her, and her heart was wrung for the lonely little boy he had once been. 'So this is a treat for you, as well as for me?' she asked lightly, and the frown between his brows vanished.

'It's turned out to be,' he agreed. 'I've been to London countless times, but I don't think I've ever sat in one of its parks before.' His mouth twisted suddenly. 'It makes me wonder if I've turned out to be just like my parents after all. I just hope I'm a better father.'

So he and Astra were planning to have children. Daisy felt the thought settle like something cold inside her. It would be Astra who would be mother to Seth's children, and Astra who would make sure that they had a happier childhood than their father. She bent her head and plucked mindlessly at the grass, afraid that Seth would be able to read her expression. 'That will be up to you and Astra,' she said tonelessly.

There was a tiny silence. Seth hadn't taken his eyes off the boys, who had managed to launch their boat at last. 'Yes, I suppose it will,' he said, but he didn't sound convinced.

Daisy had expected the ubiquitous George to drive them down to Gloucestershire the next day, but it seemed that he had been given a well-deserved weekend off. Instead, Seth drove a sleekly beautiful sports car which had appeared miraculously at the entrance to the hotel as they were about to leave. It smelt of leather and wood and money, Daisy thought, sniffing surreptitiously, and had a huge purring engine beneath the polished bonnet.

Much good it did them for the first hour. It was a perfect June morning, and everyone else in London was apparently determined to head for a weekend in the west as well. Seth muttered under his breath as they crawled

through the traffic which was jammed right out along
the M4, but it cleared eventually and he gave the big car
its head. Daisy felt the pressure in the small of her back
as it leapt forward, but it was so smooth and silent that
they hardly seemed to be moving at all.

Her spirits rose as they turned off the motorway at
last and glided along the narrow Cotswold lanes. The
hedgerows were lush with fresh grass and cow parsley,
and the villages basked golden and tranquil in the sun.
It was such a beautiful day that it was impossible not to
feel happy.

Not that she had been feeling *un*happy, Daisy caught
herself up quickly. She had absolutely nothing to feel
unhappy about. Dinner last night had gone off well and
no one had suspected that she and Seth weren't a genuine couple, although Seth hadn't touched her at all.

Of course, it wouldn't have been appropriate for them
to be all over each other at a dinner party but, still, Daisy
thought, he might have been a bit more affectionate. He
had hardly come near her all evening, in fact, and—not
wanting to be accused of not playing her part properly
again—she had taken his hand at the end of the evening
as they had made their farewells. Seth hadn't said anything, but as soon as they were outside he had dropped
her hand very deliberately.

Now Daisy slid a glance at him under her lashes. His
hands were relaxed and assured on the wheel but his
face had worn that guarded expression ever since they
had returned from the park yesterday evening, and she
couldn't help feeling a little piqued. Sitting on the grass
together, she had been convinced that he was growing
to like her for herself but now she wasn't so sure. It
wasn't that he was unpleasant, just withdrawn. Daisy
gave an inward sigh. On the whole she thought she pre-

ferred Seth when he was being disagreeable. At least she knew where she was with him then.

Still, the sun was shining, the countryside was looking beautiful and Jim was feeling better. Daisy leant out of the window and breathed in the summer smell of the grass and told herself that she didn't want any more than that.

Her good humour lasted until they arrived at Croston Park, a lovely seventeenth-century manor built of the distinctive golden-grey Cotswold stone, and were shown to their room. Stupidly Daisy hadn't even thought about having to share a room with Seth, but it should have been obvious that Henry would tell Elizabeth to put them together. She had even been considerate enough to give them a double bed.

'It's lovely,' Daisy said faintly to Elizabeth, not daring to look at Seth.

There was no chance to talk to him before they were led back downstairs to meet the other guests, who were gathered on the terrace. Daisy hardly noticed that James Gifford-Gould was among them, merely giving everyone a distracted smile as introductions were made and sinking down into a chair. Seth sat beside her. How could he look so cool and unperturbed? The thought of sharing a bed obviously didn't bother *him* in the slightest!

Accepting a drink gratefully, Daisy tried to concentrate on the conversation but all she could think about was sliding into bed next to Seth, rolling over in her sleep, touching him. No matter how much she tried to tell herself that it wouldn't matter, even if she did brush against him, she found the thought deeply unsettling. If only she could forget how lean and hard his body had been when he'd kissed her. If only she couldn't imagine quite so clearly what it would be like to run her hands over his skin. If only she could stop thinking about it!

It should have been an idyllic situation, sitting on a terrace like this with its view over an exquisite garden and the meadows beyond and only the sound of doves to compete with the laughter round the table. Daisy gulped at her Pimm's. She really must pull herself together. Seth was relaxed and smiling beside her, his dark head bent intimately towards a beautiful redhead on his other side. They looked like an advertisement, Daisy thought with a pang—glamorous, exclusive, utterly confident of their style and their power and their privilege. Everyone at the table had the same glossy assurance, as if they had never had a moment's doubt in their lives, and Daisy felt suddenly crushed. She didn't belong with these people, she realised in sudden panic.

Something must have shown in her face, for James caught her eye and gave her an encouraging smile. She smiled back gratefully, and immediately Seth's head jerked round.

'All right, honey?' he asked, running his finger down her cheek in a caress, but only Daisy could see the warning look in his eyes.

She forced another smile. 'Of course.'

Lunch was interminable. Everyone was gossiping about famous people they were apparently on first name terms with. Seth was the centre of attention. Daisy could see all the women eyeing him surreptitiously, obviously trying to work out just how committed he was to her. He wasn't withdrawn with *them*, she thought sourly, watching him exerting the charm that he never wasted on her. Any one of them would be delighted to be sharing a bed with him tonight.

Feeling twitchy again, Daisy shifted in her chair. It was mid-afternoon, lunch had finished hours ago and Henry was still opening bottles of wine. It looked as if they were going to sit here all day. Murmuring an excuse, she pushed back her chair but they were all too busy talking to notice her leave.

It was a relief to get away on her own. Daisy slipped around the side of the house and out of sight across the meadows to where a stream meandered between the trees. The tall grasses tickled her bare legs and she picked her way carefully to avoid the flowers. She was wearing a silky summer dress that felt cool and comfortable in the sun, and she took off her shoes so that she could sit by the stream and dangle her feet in the water.

The stillness of the hot afternoon was irresistibly soothing. On the far side of the stream some cows were grazing in the meadow, knee-deep in grass, and a couple of horses flicked their tails in the shade, but otherwise there was only the soft call of wood pigeons and the ripple of the water as Daisy wriggled her toes in the stream. Gradually the edgy feeling faded. It was stupid to get so worked up about sharing a bed with Seth. If the prospect didn't bother him why should it bother her? It would only be for a night, after all, and Seth had made it very clear over the last twenty-four hours that he had no interest in her other than as a diversion from his real affair with Astra.

Daisy thought of how at home he had looked on that terrace, part of a charmed, impenetrable circle of wealth and glamour. That was where he belonged—not sitting in a public park eating ice-cream—and it was time that she just accepted it.

It was one thing to accept it and quite another to waste a hot afternoon feeling awkward and out of place. Deciding that the exclusive group on the terrace wouldn't miss her anyway, Daisy stood up and told herself that she was quite content to be alone with the sun on her shoulders and the soft grass beneath her bare feet.

Her shoes dangled from her hand as she wandered aimlessly along the banks of the stream until she came at last to a mown field, where six children of varying sizes were playing rounders and arguing vociferously about whose turn it was to bat.

Daisy watched them for a while, unable to help comparing their enthusiasm with the languid sophistication of her fellow-guests, and when a tennis ball came sailing through the air towards her she dropped her shoes and caught it automatically. A boy of about twelve who had thrown down the bat and was haring around the improvised bases looked furious at being caught out, but the other children were obviously delighted and Daisy was promptly conscripted as a fielder.

It wasn't long before they were all firm friends. Daisy was less successful as a bowler but the children magnanimously offered her the bat instead, and she was well on her way to making a complete round after a particularly fine shot when the ball was lobbed neatly into the baseball cap that was acting as fourth base just before she reached it.

'You're out! You're out!' The children were dancing up and down with excitement. Ready to pretend to complain bitterly at such accurate fielding, Daisy looked laughingly around to see Seth watching her with amusement from the edge of the field.

She stopped laughing abruptly, and her heart did an extraordinary somersault at the unexpected sight of him. For a moment she could only stand stock-still and stare back at him across the grass. The sheer impact of his presence was undeniable, even from a distance, and as he walked towards her everything about him seemed very sharply defined against the blue sky—the hard, exciting planes of his face, the solid outline of his lean body, the balanced, easy way he moved. He was wearing cream trousers and a dark blue polo shirt, and somehow managed to look just as much as if he belonged here, surrounded by children, as he had done on the terrace with the pampered and the privileged.

Daisy was suddenly acutely conscious of her red face, bare feet and dishevelled hair. 'Hello,' she said a little warily, wishing that this breathless feeling could be attributed solely to the rounders. 'What are you doing here?'

'Looking for you,' said Seth. 'I wondered where you were.'

'I just felt like a walk.' Daisy knew that she sounded defensive, but she couldn't help it.

The children were getting impatient at the interruption to the game. 'We're playing rounders,' the smallest girl informed Seth. 'Do you want to play?'

To Daisy's astonishment, Seth smiled down at the little girl and said that he did. 'Rounders is like baseball, right?'

He probably knew exactly what rounders was, Daisy realised, absurdly touched by the way he let the children laboriously explain the rules to him. Knowing what she did about his own experience of growing up, she hadn't expected him to be so natural with children. They were all crowded round him now, telling him how hopeless Daisy had been as a bowler.

'I'll see if I can do better than Daisy, shall I?' said Seth, and grinned wickedly over their heads to where Daisy stood, wishing that he wouldn't keep confusing her by being nice just when she had decided that she wasn't going to waste any more time thinking about him.

Patiently he bowled to all the children, making sure that they had the chance to make a run. Daisy was relegated back to a fielding position, but she was so distracted by Seth that she kept fumbling catches. She just hoped that Seth thought that she was doing it deliberately to give the little ones a chance.

In the ruthless way of children it had been decided that smallest, a little boy called Rory who couldn't have been more than five, should go last. Seth tossed him endless gentle balls until at last he managed to take a swipe at it. Determined to make sure that he made a run, Daisy made a show of dropping the ball while the other children cried out in disgust and then threw it wildly in Seth's direction so that he had no hope of catching it. Retrieving it, he aimed the ball carefully so that it just missed the last post as Rory panted home, beaming. Unnoticed by the children, who were already squabbling over who was to go next, Seth and Daisy smiled at each other.

Seth's smile set a strange sensation strumming inside Daisy. It was warm and sweet and infinitely disturbing and, after a moment, her own smile faded uncertainly and she looked away.

They walked back through the meadows together in silence. The children had been disappointed to see them go, but their shouts could still be heard receding into the distance. 'Nice kids,' said Seth after a while.

'Yes.' Daisy sounded subdued. She was agonisingly aware of Seth beside her. She had slipped on her shoes, and now her hands felt empty and awkward. The one nearest Seth kept tingling, and Daisy was so afraid that it might reach out of its own volition and curl around his fingers that she folded her arms across her chest and tucked both hands firmly away.

There was another long silence. 'Why didn't you tell me where you were going?' asked Seth eventually.

Daisy shrugged. 'I didn't think you'd notice if I was there or not.'

'I always notice.'

Her eyes slid away from his. 'It would have broken up the party if I'd announced that I was going for a walk,' she said a little sulkily.

'It broke up the party anyway,' said Seth with something of a snap. 'When it was obvious that you weren't coming back James Gifford-Gould decided that *he'd* like a walk as well, and then I had to go for a walk, too, to make sure that he wasn't thinking of walking in the same direction as you.'

'I could hardly have arranged an assignation with him since we've been here,' protested Daisy. 'I haven't had a chance to see him on my own, even if I had wanted to!'

Seth's mouth was set in an unyielding line. 'You'd better make sure the opportunity doesn't arise,' he said coldly. 'From now on, I want you to stay right where I can keep an eye on you.'

He seemed much more intent on keeping a close eye on Miranda, Daisy thought sourly at the ball later that evening, watching Seth dance past with the beautiful redhead yet again. He had hardly taken his eyes off her all evening. For someone so determined not to let Daisy out of his sight, he was giving a very good impression of ignoring her completely.

Daisy herself had kept a bright smile pinned to her face all evening, and her jaw was beginning to ache. The afternoon's tranquillity had evaporated completely. It was very easy to make resolutions about not getting involved; less easy to keep them when Seth managed to unnerve her just by being there. Daisy had been very conscious of the intimacy of the situation as she and Seth had changed in their room before dinner. Neither of them had mentioned the fact that they would have to share a bed later.

She had sat at the dressing-table and tried to concentrate on not making a mess of her make-up, but Seth's reflection had kept catching at her eye as he moved around the room. He had come out of the bathroom wearing only trousers, and Daisy's mascara wand had slipped at the first sight of his strong, sleek brown chest behind her. Her heart had thudded uncomfortably at the base of her throat as she'd scrubbed away the smudge of mascara and started again. Anyone would think she had never seen a male body before!

Seth had seemed quite unaware of the fact that she had been studying him covertly in the mirror. His back had been turned as he'd pulled a shirt out of the wardrobe and, for a dizzying moment, Daisy had let herself imagine what it would be like to cross the room and trace the line of his spine with tantalising fingers; to know that he would turn at her touch and smile and draw her into the hard warmth of his body...

Daisy put the mascara down on the dressing-table with a sharp click. Why on earth had she allowed herself to think about *that*? Edgily she began brushing her dark curls, but it was impossible not to be aware of Seth moving about the room—buttoning his shirt, fixing in his cuff-links, adjusting his bow tie.

Suddenly his reflection appeared directly behind hers as he shrugged himself into his jacket. Daisy would have given anything to have been able to continue brushing her hair unconcernedly but, against her will, her eyes met Seth's in the mirror and the brush faltered. For a long, long moment they just looked at each other's reflection while the silence gathered into a vibrating tension.

He was standing right behind her. It would be easy for him to put his hands on her shoulders; so easy for her to lean back against him and to tip up her face for his kiss. Daisy laid the brush down very carefully onto the dressing-table, her fingers clenched around the handle with the effort of not swaying back in instinctive invitation. It wouldn't have been welcome—that was obvious. Seth's eyes held that guarded look again and he made no move to touch her, simply asking her if she was ready.

'Don't I look ready?' Daisy's tone was sharp with a disappointment that she refused to admit, and she rose from the stool with a rustle of watered silk. She was wearing a ball gown with full skirts and a wide collar that left her shoulders bare. The deep, rich blue almost exactly matched her eyes, throwing into relief her fragile bones and the pale luminosity of her skin.

'You look fine,' said Seth after a moment. His expression was unreadable but there was just the faintest undercurrent of strain in his voice.

Fine? Was that all he could say? Conscious of a sense of pique, Daisy made a big show of dropping her lipstick into her bag and snapping it shut. She was damned if she was going to let him see how stung she was by his lack of enthusiasm. 'I'm sorry if I'm not up to your usual standard of escort, but you'll just have to put up with me. It won't be for much longer, I hope.'

'Perhaps not,' said Seth, holding the door with mock courtesy. 'But, until I say so, our agreement still holds so I hope you're not going to forget what I said earlier? I don't want you sneaking off with James Gifford-Gould the moment my back's turned.'

'I haven't forgotten who's paying me, if that's what you're worrying about,' said Daisy crossly. 'I'll be the perfect girlfriend, and make sure that everyone knows that I've only got eyes for you.'

'Just make sure you do,' said Seth.

Now Daisy watched Seth and Miranda with a smouldering eye. How was she supposed to act devoted when the object of her devotion could hardly be bothered to acknowledge her existence? He was the one who was so keen to convince everyone that he was in love with her, after all. The least he could do was to dance with her the way he was dancing with Miranda. There was no need for him to hold her quite that closely, surely? If anyone was going to cling to Seth and smile adoringly up into his face, Daisy decided, it ought to be *her*.

Everyone else in the party was already beginning to give her pitying looks. It must be obvious to them all that Seth had transferred his interest to Miranda, who was so much better suited to him and who looked so much more than just 'fine'. Daisy's temper, which had been simmering all evening, was beginning to flicker dangerously.

By the time Seth and Miranda returned to the table Daisy had had enough. If Seth wanted her to act like an adoring girlfriend that's what she would do, and she would make sure that Miranda knew whose man he was while she was at it! Coming up unnoticed behind Seth's chair, she slid her arms around his neck and bent to kiss his ear.

'You've done all your duty dances,' she murmured softly, but loud enough for Miranda to hear. 'It's my turn now.'

Seth had tensed at the first touch of her lips, and Daisy could feel the rigidity of his jaw as she pressed slow, seductive kisses along his cheek to the corner of his mouth. 'You've been dancing all evening,' he said in an oddly unsteady voice. 'Aren't you tired?'

Enraged by his unenthusiastic response, Daisy inched her lips closer to his. 'We don't need to dance,' she said in her sultry temptress voice, but her blue eyes were bright with challenge. 'You can just hold me.'

'Who could resist an invitation like that?' said

Miranda with a brittle laugh, and Seth pushed back his chair.

'Who, indeed?' he said and, taking Daisy's hand, pulled her onto the dance floor and into his arms. 'What do you think you're playing at?' he muttered through clenched teeth, bending his head as if to lay his cheek against hers.

'I'm earning my money,' said Daisy, twining her arms around his neck with a dangerously bright smile. 'You were very insistent that I should behave like the perfect girlfriend this evening.'

'Couldn't you manage it without that embarrassing public display? I practically had to peel you off me!'

Daisy was unrepentant. 'It was the only way I could get your attention,' she pointed out. 'I suppose you'd rather I'd sent you a note?'

'Don't be ridiculous,' said Seth irritably. 'If you'd wanted to dance all you had to do was ask.'

'How was I supposed to do that when you've made a point of ignoring me all evening?'

'I haven't been ignoring you!'

'Then how come I had to practically seduce you to get you to dance with me?' asked Daisy. Over Seth's shoulder she could see Miranda watching them resentfully, and assumed what she hoped was a blissful smile.

'Because, whenever I looked for you, you seemed more than happy to be surrounded by men,' said Seth in a cold voice.

'How would you know?' she demanded crossly. 'You've been glued to Miranda all evening. I mean, if we're going to talk about embarrassing displays in public...'

'I have not been glued to Miranda, as you put it,' Seth began furiously, but Daisy interrupted him by pulling his head down to hers.

'Smile, *darling*,' she reminded him provocatively, and risked a kiss to the pulse that hammered just below his ear. 'Remember how much in love we are!'

Seth sucked in his breath and clearly concentrated on mentally counting to ten. 'Why do you always have to exaggerate?' he said between gritted teeth after a moment. 'You're either disappearing off on your own or all over me like a rash. Why can't you just behave normally?'

'Because I have no idea what normal *is*, as far as you're concerned! One minute you're banging on and on about me acting like a besotted girlfriend, and the next you're complaining because I'm behaving like any *normal* girl would behave if she'd seen her man carrying on the way you've been carrying on with Miranda tonight!'

Daisy was incensed at the injustice of Seth's accusation, but she was equally furious with herself for noticing the strength of his body. Her lips were throbbing with the feel of his skin where she had kissed him, and the almost irresistible urge to press her face into his throat and kiss him again was merely fuelling her anger.

'It would make it a lot easier for me if you'd make up your mind what you want,' she went on, still with that idiotic smile pinned to her face. 'You say you want to convince everyone that we're in love but if no one believes it it won't be *my* fault, so don't blame me when your rotten pre-nuptial contract falls through!'

Seth opened his mouth to reply, but at that moment the dance ended and Henry was beckoning them off the floor. Everyone else, it seemed, was ready to go and the party was heading back to Croston Park. Frustrated at being stopped in mid-argument, Seth and Daisy had to contain themselves until they were alone in their room—

by which stage both were much too cross to feel awkward about the immediate prospect of sharing a bed.

'I hope you're satisfied!' snapped Seth as soon as the door closed behind them. 'If anyone thought we were in love before they certainly won't think so now after that little performance!'

'*What* little performance?' said Daisy dangerously.

'You hardly said a word on the way back,' he accused her.

'What did you want me to say with Bill and Sarah in the car?'

'You could have made it a little less obvious that we'd been interrupted in the middle of a row!'

'There wasn't much point in me trying to do that when you were sitting there with a face like concrete!' Daisy was angrily jerking out her earrings. 'I'm fed up with doing all the work. How can I possibly pretend to be in love with you when you treat me like some kind of servant? Do this; don't do that...I don't know why you're bothering with this stupid charade, anyway. No one in their right minds would ever suspect that anyone as rude and arrogant as you was capable of being in love, and as for persuading them that there was anything remotely even *likeable* about you, well, anyone who could act that convincingly would deserve an Oscar!'

One of Seth's eyelids twitched ominously as he ripped off his bow-tie. 'You could practically buy an Oscar with what I'm paying you to do just that,' he said. 'Or had you forgotten that little matter of money you're so keen to get your hands on?'

'I'm hardly likely to forget that,' retorted Daisy as she snatched up her nightdress. 'Can you think of any reason other than money for me to climb into bed beside you?'

Before Seth could reply she had slammed into the bathroom and locked the door.

When she emerged she was wearing the oyster satin nightdress, and carrying the ball gown before her like a shield. Stubborn chin stuck in the air, she ignored Seth completely and marched over to the wardrobe to hang up the dress.

Seth gave an exclamation of disgust, and shut himself in the bathroom in his turn. Daisy quickly turned off the light and leapt into bed, drawing the duvet right up to her chin. Perhaps if she didn't actually see Seth getting in beside her she could pretend that he wasn't there at all.

Of course, as soon as he came out he switched on one of the bedside lights. It threw a soft glow over the room, but Daisy screwed up her eyes as if at a spotlight. 'I'm trying to get to sleep!' she protested.

'Close your eyes,' Seth suggested callously. 'I don't see why I should have to grope round in the dark.' He stopped short as he saw where Daisy was lying. 'That's my side of the bed!'

Daisy didn't care which side of the bed she slept on, but she was in no mood to compromise. 'Tough!' she said succinctly. 'I was here first.'

'Don't you ever stop fighting?' he sighed in exasperation as he unbuttoned his shirt.

'Don't you ever stop insisting on having your own way?'

'No,' said Seth. 'I always get my own way.' Dropping his shirt onto a chair, he sat down on the side of the bed right next to her and calmly began to take off his shoes and socks. 'You should know that by now.'

He was trying to intimidate her into moving over. Daisy could see the muscles rippling in the broad shoulders; could feel the warmth and solidity of his body through the duvet. Hastily she transferred her gaze to the ceiling. This was *not* the time to start thinking about things like that. This was a battle of wills, not of bodies.

Seth turned to look down to where Daisy lay, stubbornly clutching the duvet. In the dim light her eyes were huge and dark. 'Are you going to move over, or am I to take your presence on my side of the bed as an invitation?'

CHAPTER SEVEN

'INVITATION?' Daisy sat bolt upright in indignation at the sheer conceit of the man, taking the duvet with her. 'You don't honestly think I'm likely to be offering you an invitation after the way you've been treating me all evening, do you? I'm not that stupid! You've made it very clear that an invitation from me is the last thing you'd want!'

'What did I say to make you think that?' asked Seth softly.

'It's not what you said—it's the way you react whenever I come anywhere near you,' she said sullenly. 'I'd get a warmer response from an iceberg!'

As soon as the words were out she knew that they had been a mistake. Seth's eyes narrowed and he leant forward, placing a hand on either side of her so that she was forced to sink back down onto the pillow. 'I'm sorry I've disappointed you,' he said.

'I'm not disappointed,' said Daisy bravely, but the nearness of his body was making her feel light-headed with a mixture of nervousness and insidious excitement.

'You sounded disappointed.'

'Well, I'm not.' It was hard to sound unconcerned when his body was only inches away from hers, but Daisy did her best. 'If you don't want us to look like a convincing couple that's up to you. You're the one paying for my performance.' No harm in stressing that it *was* just a performance.

'I am, aren't I?' said Seth, rubbing one of her curls between his fingers, and something in his voice made

Daisy tense. 'And paying an extortionate sum, too. I think I'd better make sure I get my money's worth, don't you?' He leant even closer, until barely a breath separated them, clicking his tongue when Daisy tried to shrink further down into the bed. 'Now who's being the iceberg?'

'W-we're not acting now,' whispered Daisy.

'No, but it sounds to me as if you think I need a little more rehearsal.' His lips brushed teasingly over hers. 'Let's both practise a warmer response, shall we?' Now he was nibbling tiny kisses along her jaw, snarling her senses into a terrible knot of desire. Daisy's hands clenched over the edge of the duvet, and she had to force herself to lie still and fight the urge to put her arms around his neck and turn her face to find the mouth that was driving her to distraction.

'Well?' Seth murmured in her ear. 'How am I doing?'

'I…I don't think you need any more practice,' she managed to say.

Raising his head, he looked down into her face—his expression quite unreadable in the shadows. The lamplight just caught the edge of his cheek and burnished one shoulder and Daisy felt the last air leaking out of her lungs. 'You wouldn't want me to stop just when I'm getting the hang of it, would you?' he asked in a voice that was deep and warm and sent shameful anticipation reverberating through her as he bent once more and kissed her mouth.

His lips were tantalising, persuasive, unexpectedly gentle. He was still braced on his hands on either side of her, so that only their mouths were touching. Daisy knew that she could easily push him away. She knew that she *should*. But a feeling like warm honey was spreading through her, liquefying her bones and dissolving all memories of Seth's arrogance and all thought of her own anger—all awareness of anything but the terrible desire that held her in thrall. Seth could feel her melting beneath him, for his kiss deepened and somehow Daisy's hands had released the duvet and were creeping around his neck.

'You wouldn't want that, would you, Daisy?' he murmured against her lips. 'You wouldn't really want me to stop now?'

Yes: that was all she had to say. This was her chance to say that that *was* what she wanted. This was her chance to slide over to the other side of the bed and firmly turn her back. This was her chance to rescue her pride and her dignity and everything that would make her feel better tomorrow morning. All she had to say was 'yes'.

'No' whispered Daisy, and Seth smiled.

'I didn't think you would,' he said, and captured her lips once more.

This time his kiss was more insistent, but Daisy had made her decision and abandoned herself joyfully to the searing pleasure of being able to kiss him back. It was blissful to be able to explore the sleek, supple skin and trace the outline of his spine with questing fingers, just as she had imagined earlier that evening; heaven to feel his weight and his warmth and the hard demand of his body pressing her down into the bed. When Seth levered himself up enough to pull aside the duvet her only protest was at the interruption to their kisses, and it was soon muffled as he secured her against him once more.

His sure hands were smoothing over the satin nightdress like fire, rucking it up as they possessed her body with increasing urgency. Daisy gasped as his fingers drifted, discovered, scorched a trail of excitement over her skin and, heady with pleasure, she rolled Seth over so that he lay beneath her. The soft yellow glow of the lamp spilled over them as if they were one, catching the sheen of skin or the curve of limb but otherwise cradling them in shadows. Nothing existed beyond that small circle of lamplight. They were alone in the darkness where all that mattered was touch and feel and the beckoning promise of fulfilment.

It was Daisy's turn to bend and tease Seth with slow, slow kisses, starting at his mouth and drifting enticingly downwards from the base of his throat to follow the arrowing V of crisp hairs on his chest until she reached his trousers. Undoing the first button, she paused and smiled wickedly up at him. 'You wouldn't want me to stop now, would you?'

'No,' said Seth with a ragged laugh, swinging her beneath him once more, and his lips whispered over her skin. 'No, I wouldn't.'

He peeled the nightdress up over her head and dropped it to the floor with a slither of satin which was followed by the rustle of his trousers, and then at last there was the gasping sensation of skin on skin that was as a spark to the explosion of excitement that rocketed between them. Their kisses grew hungry, their hands harder and more compelling as they explored each other with a new urgency.

Daisy was afire, adrift in a swinging, spinning desire that swirled higher and higher with every touch of Seth's body. He was so strong, so solid, so secure. She wanted to burrow feverishly into the unyielding firmness of him; to cling to him as an anchor against the rolling, rushing, turbulent tide of passion that threatened to snatch her away from anything she had ever known before.

So strong was the feeling that she cried out Seth's name in a mixture of panic and need, but he was there already—in her and around her. After the first moment of exquisite relief they began to move together to the urgent, insistent pulse of desire, slowly at first, murmuring each other's names, then faster as the hunger gathered momentum with every breath they took. Wrapping herself around him, Daisy dug her fingers into Seth's back, beyond speaking, beyond thinking—beyond anything but a blind trust in him to take her with him.

And he did, guiding her up a dizzying spiral of longing until even he lost control at last and they could only cling together as they were swept along by a force that was stronger than both of them. Irresistible, indescribable, it surged on and up to a heart-stopping climax, leaving them poised almost unbearably on the very brink of ecstasy, before sending them hurtling into an explosion of sensation that left them shuddering in each other's arms.

A very long time later Daisy opened her eyes to realise that her fingers were still digging into Seth's shoulders. Very slowly she released them, and ran her hands blissfully over his back. She felt a boundless, golden sense of plenitude, unlike anything she had ever felt before, as if the tension which had knotted her ever since she first met Seth had been disentangled and smoothed into enchantment.

Seth's face was buried in her hair. He lay heavily on her, but she didn't care. She could feel his shoulders rise and fall as his ragged breathing slowed and steadied—until he stirred at last and rolled over, taking her with him and rolling her over again until she ended up on the far side of the bed.

'The lengths some people go to get their own way!' Daisy teased.

'The things some people will do rather than give in graciously!' Seth retorted, kissing her throat and running his hands possessively over her curves.

Daisy tried to look aggrieved, but her mouth kept curling upwards in a contented smile. 'I liked it where I was,' she pretended to grumble.

'I liked it where you were too,' he smiled. 'Do I take it that you think my performance has improved?'

'Well...' She assumed a considering look, but when Seth tickled her she gave in and smiled back. 'It wasn't bad for an iceberg, I suppose!'

'Iceberg! How could any man be an iceberg with you around, Daisy?'

'You were doing a pretty good job before,' Daisy pointed out, stretching luxuriously beneath his lazily drifting hands.

'That's what you think,' said Seth enigmatically, and settled her more comfortably into his side. They lay for a while in contented silence, listening to each other breathing. Resting her head against his shoulder, Daisy traced slow circles on his stomach with her fingertips while his hand smoothed almost reflectively up and down her arm. She could feel the steady, infinitely re-assuring rise and fall of his chest, and breathed in the scent of his skin with a shiver of joy.

Seth felt the quiver run through her. 'You're not cold, are you?'

'No, I'm not cold,' she said softly, but he reached over anyway to switch off the lamp and pull the duvet around them.

Cradled by darkness and silence and enfolded in Seth's arms—conscious only of him warm and breathing beside her—Daisy felt as if she had reached home after a long and tortuous journey. Utterly relaxed together, they drifted in and out of sleep—stirring occasionally for a mumbled kiss before settling themselves close once more.

The hostility which had flared between them after the ball seemed a lifetime ago, but it had been late then and the summer night was so short that it was only a couple of hours before the dawn light began to disperse the friendly darkness. Daisy surfaced to the sound of frantically twittering birds outside the window and the feel of Seth's deep, slow breathing on the back of her neck. She ran her hand down the arm that lay possessively around her, holding her into the long, hard curve of his body even in sleep, drifted over the fine, dark hairs on his forearm and traced the bones in his wrist, lovingly entwining her fingers with those which had given her so much heart-stopping pleasure.

She didn't want it to be morning. She wanted the night to go on and on so that they could lie like this for ever, instead of facing the reality of day. Reality meant remembering Astra and just what she was doing with Seth in this comfortable bed. Daisy wasn't a fool. She knew that she could never compare with the dazzling, talented, beautiful Astra. Astra and Seth were two of a kind—they belonged together in a world that had no connection to Daisy's. They might have called off their relationship for now, but that was only temporary. Why else would Seth have insisted on Daisy being with him still under false pretences?

The joy they had discovered together in the diminishing darkness could never last, Daisy realised sadly. All the differences between them, which had dissolved as soon as he touched her, stood out clearer than ever in the dawn light.

There was no use thinking that last night would mean anything special to Seth. He was a man, and she had been there. She might distract him for a while; she might amuse him, but she could never hope to share his life. For these few weeks they were together, but a few weeks was all it would ever be before he and Astra sorted things out or he found another girl who belonged in his world in a way that Daisy could never do.

A few short weeks... They would go to the Caribbean soon, and then she would have to find Tom. It would be easier to make the break, having a reason to go. Daisy was determined not to be difficult or demanding. When the deal was over she would walk away without a backward look, but in the meantime...

In the meantime Seth's hand was drifting over her stomach and up to her breast and the old, helpless, bone-melting desire was stirring again. If she only had a short time with him should she not make the best of it?

He was mumbling kisses along her shoulder. 'What are you thinking about?' he murmured against her skin.

Daisy stretched and rolled over to face him with a smile. Putting her arms round his neck, she began to press kisses up his throat in her turn. 'I was just thinking that if we wanted to carry on convincing people that we were lovers we could really do with another rehearsal...'

'That's funny,' said Seth as his mouth inched lower. 'That's just what I was thinking too.'

Daisy floated through the day in a glow of contentment. She supposed that she smiled and chatted and made polite conversation with those who weren't nursing monumental hangovers, but her whole awareness was focused on Seth. He hardly touched her at all, just the occasional graze of his fingers along her arm or the brush of his knee, but every now and then their eyes would meet and they would exchange a private smile that sent the champagne of happiness fizzing along her veins.

They drove back to London through a glorious golden evening. Long shadows slanted across the fields and striped the narrow Cotswold lanes, flickering over the speeding car. Daisy felt bathed in sunlight. Leaning back in her seat, she stretched her arms above her head and sighed with contentment before turning her head in time to catch the sudden blaze of expression in Seth's eyes. It left her feeling oddly winded and there was a taut moment of silence as he looked back to the road.

'You look very pleased with yourself,' he said, but his voice didn't sound quite like himself.

Daisy drew a rather shaky breath. 'Just getting into my role,' she rejoined as lightly as she could.

Seth threw her another quick glance. 'Shall we stop and have something to eat instead of going straight back to London?' he asked abruptly.

'I thought you told Henry you had to get back?'

'I was just tired of sitting around being polite to people.' He shrugged.

'So you want to sit around being rude to me instead?' said Daisy innocently, and Seth laughed.

'I'll be nice,' he promised. 'Well, what do you say?'

The strange moment of tension had gone. Daisy smiled and settled back into her seat once more. 'I'd love to,' she said.

They found a quiet pub by a river and sat side by side at a table outside, watching the ducks dabbling in the still water. The food was indifferent, but Daisy didn't care what she ate. It was enough to sit next to Seth in the golden gathering dusk and feel their thighs just touching on the wooden slatted bench. In spite of the simmering awareness between them, they talked easily together until she asked when they would be going out to the Caribbean.

There was a small silence. 'I'd forgotten you were so keen to get out there,' said Seth expressionlessly. 'What is it you want to do there that you can't do here?'

'I'm looking for somebody,' said Daisy. She hesitated. 'I...I hadn't forgotten that we had a deal, Seth.'

'Did you think that *I* had?'

'No.' She drew a deep breath. It had to be said, and it might as well be now when their faces were half-hidden in the dusk. 'I just wanted you to know that I didn't take last night too seriously. I know this is just a temporary situation. I've got plans of my own in the Caribbean, so you needn't worry about me being difficult to get rid of when you and Astra...well, when you don't need me any more.'

It was impossible to tell what Seth was thinking, but she was sure that he must be relieved that she wasn't going to involve him in any emotional scenes. Daisy twisted her glass between her hands, unable to look at him directly. 'You're paying me to pretend to be in love with you and that's what I'll do. I...I just thought that since rehearsals were going so well...'

She trailed off. 'Yes?' said Seth, his voice giving absolutely nothing away.

'Well...that we should make the most of them.' She had got so far that she might as well carry on now, Daisy decided. 'We've both got other commitments,' she ploughed on doggedly when Seth still didn't say anything. 'We both know exactly where we stand. But while we *do* have to be together we might as well enjoy it.' She was trying to sound carelessly sophisticated, but Seth's silence was unnerving her. 'If you want to, of course,' she finished lamely.

'No strings attached?'

'None. It would just be for the next few weeks together, exactly as we agreed, and then we'd go our separate ways with no hard feelings on either side.'

There was another long, nerve-wracking silence. Perhaps she'd overdone the casualness? But everything she knew about Seth told her that he would withdraw at the first suggestion of clinging or messy emotion and, as he hesitated, Daisy discovered exactly how much she wanted him to agree. It wouldn't be for ever, but she would take whatever he had to give.

In the twilight Seth's expression was unreadable. She could feel his eyes on her averted face and realised in sudden panic that he was just trying to find the words to refuse her kindly. He was going to tell her that last night had been a mistake; that they should try and keep their relationship on a purely business level.

At last Seth reached out and thoughtfully twisted one of her curls round his finger. Daisy steeled herself for the disappointment.

'You've got yourself another deal, Daisy Deare,' he said, and she caught her breath in relief, turning to look at him as if to reassure herself that he wasn't teasing. 'Don't look so surprised,' said Seth, and his smile gleamed through the dusky light. 'You didn't really think I'd turn down an offer like that, did you?'

Daisy's face lit with an answering smile. 'I hope you wouldn't,' she said honestly, and leant into his kiss with a sigh of release, unprepared even after last night for the electric charge of excitement as their lips met. The kiss went on and on until Seth drew away with a shaky laugh. 'Come on,' he said, taking her hand and pulling her to her feet. 'Let's go.'

Back in the suite in London they undressed each other with fumbling fingers, leaving a trail of clothes on their way to the bedroom. Half laughing, half frenzied, they fell onto the bed, rolling together with deep, desperate kisses until the laughter faded and they were left with only the wild, rocketing excitement and the intensity of need that consumed them both. They couldn't touch each other enough; couldn't hold each other close enough as they abandoned themselves to the blistering uprush of desire. It swept over them and through them, plunging unstoppably on to a glorious starburst of release that rocked the world on its axis and made them cry out together in wonder and in awe.

Later, much later, they made love again but this time with a piercing lack of haste. Daisy had never known that the touch of lips and hands and bodies could be so inexpressibly sweet; had never imagined that Seth was capable of such tenderness. When she lay in his arms afterwards she found that slow tears were rolling down her cheeks. Seth wiped them away with his thumb in a caress that wrung her heart. 'I know,' he whispered softly and held her close. 'I know.'

'You haven't forgotten that a journalist from one of the London dailies is due here at eleven o'clock, have you?' Maria had been giving Seth curious looks ever since she had arrived promptly that morning only to find out, instead of having been hard at work for a good two hours already, he was still having breakfast with Daisy.

'Damn! I had.' Seth drained his coffee-cup as he got to his feet. 'There's a few things I want to do before he comes, too.' He tangled his fingers in Daisy's hair. 'Will you be all right on your own this morning?' he asked almost roughly, and she smiled serenely up at him.

'Of course.'

'It might be an idea if you were around when this journalist turns up,' he went on. 'I think the rumour's got around pretty well by now, but it wouldn't do any harm to have your existence confirmed in print.'

The tiniest shadow touched Daisy's happiness at the reminder of her real role, but she immediately took herself to task. She had known the score all along. She couldn't complain about it now.

'I'll be here,' she said.

The journalist turned out to be a deceptively fresh-faced young man with very sharp eyes. When Daisy had heard his name she had grimaced. Stephen Rickman had a reputation for incisive interviews and a knack of cutting through the verbiage to the heart of the matter. If they could convince him they could convince anyone.

Stephen Rickman had obviously heard the rumours and didn't seem at all surprised to find Daisy pouring out the coffee. He had a pleasant, unassuming manner, but she was sure that he noticed every detail as she sat next to Seth on the sofa. 'Shall I leave you to get on with the interview?' she asked when the initial courtesies were over. She had half risen, but Seth reached out lazily and pulled her back down beside him.

'Why don't you stay?' he said with a grin. 'You can stop me getting into trouble.'

'Yes, do stay,' urged Stephen Rickman. 'I'd like to talk to you, too, if I may.'

Daisy was nervous at first, but as Stephen and Seth seemed to be getting on well she gradually relaxed and began to contribute her own comments. It seemed more of a conversation than an interview, she thought. Seth was humorously crisp and authoritative, deflecting any awkward questions and justifying controversial decisions he had made with the ease of long practice.

When Stephen turned at last from business to Seth's personal reputation it was obvious that he was expecting a rebuff and was taken aback to find that, contrary to his reputation, Seth was perfectly affable, although he did manage to answer every question without revealing anything at all that wasn't already on record. Daisy was less experienced, but she fended off questions about their relationship with as much aplomb as she could muster while Seth's hand, unseen by Stephen, was playing distractingly up and down her spine.

'Seth Carrington is a man of awesome wealth and power,' said Stephen at last. 'He also has—if I may say so—a reputation for ruthlessness in both his business and his personal dealings. What's it like to be in love with a man like that?'

Daisy looked at Seth. His fingers were still smoothing over her back, but the grey eyes held a lurking smile as they met hers. She thought about what she had read of him; about the callousness and the arrogance and the harshness she had seen in him. And then she thought about how he had sat on the grass and told her of his childhood; about how careful he had been to let a little boy complete his run without making it obvious that he had helped; about how he had held her last night and wiped the tears from her cheeks. The realisation of how much she loved him hit her with the force of a blow.

Stephen's question reverberated in the air as Daisy looked into Seth's eyes, her own dark and suddenly uncertain. What was it like to be in love with Seth? It was alarming; it was hopeless; it was irresistibly, terrifyingly glorious and rapturous and *right*. It was knowing that life was brighter and richer for having met him and loved him, just as it would be unutterably empty without him.

'It…' To her horror, Daisy's voice cracked as she began to answer and she had to clear her throat. 'It's wonderful to be in love with anyone,' she managed at last.

'But is there anything special about Seth?'

Daisy hadn't taken her gaze from Seth. 'Everything about him is special to me,' she said softly.

The photographer arrived shortly afterwards and shot off reels of film. 'Can we try one of the two of you together?' he called, and Daisy moved obediently close to Seth. She could feel him getting impatient and fluttered her eyelashes up at him with an exaggeratedly soulful look which she knew would make him laugh. It did, and she laughed with him, and for a timeless moment they forgot the camera and the photographer and the watching journalist.

'Great!' said the photographer in satisfaction. 'I reckon that'll do it.'

Seth released Daisy reluctantly and turned to Stephen. 'When's the interview coming out?'

'Tomorrow, I hope,' said Stephen. 'I'll send you a copy, of course. Will you still be in London?'

'No,' said Seth, to Daisy's astonishment. 'I'm taking Daisy to Cutlass Cay tomorrow. You can fax a copy to me there.'

As soon as they had left Daisy pounced on Seth. 'You didn't tell me that we were going to the Caribbean tomorrow!' she accused him.

'I've only just decided,' he said. 'I had thought we might go to Paris tomorrow and then on to Cutlass from there, but there's no reason why we shouldn't go straight there—unless you'd rather stick to cities?'

'Oh, no,' said Daisy quickly. She knew that she should feel more enthusiastic at the prospect of reaching her goal at last, but all she could think was that the sooner she got to the Caribbean the sooner this arrangement with Seth would be over. 'No, I'd like to go to the island.'

Why had she let herself fall in love with him when she had *known* how hopeless it would be? It was going to make it so much harder to leave. How naïve she had been to think that she would be able to calmly walk away from Seth without regrets!

No strings, she had promised him, and she would keep that promise. 'H-how long were you planning to stay?' she asked, to reassure him that she hadn't forgotten the terms they had agreed.

Seth didn't look at her. 'I guess it depends on Astra,'

he said after a minute, and it was almost as if he was trying to reassure *her* as well that there were still no strings attached to their deal as far as he was concerned. 'We had planned that after you and I had been there a few days she would come over as one of a party. If there were enough people there, and you'd been established as my main interest, we thought there would be plenty of opportunities to be alone together without anyone suspecting anything.' His voice was flat, as if the prospect didn't enthuse him.

'I see.' Daisy wanted to go over to him and slip her arms around him and beg him not to invite anyone else, least of all Astra, but she couldn't do that. 'I know this is just a temporary situation,' she had told him. She would make no claim on him, or ask him for something he couldn't give. 'Once Astra has been I presume I'll be free to leave?' she asked steadily.

'If that's what you want.' Seth's face was closed, and the tension jangled in the silence. 'You've obviously got your own plans.'

Daisy forced herself to think about Jim and her mother. She had made them a promise, too, and she couldn't abandon her search for Tom just to stay on with Seth for a few more days, a few more weeks, until he tired of her or until Astra decided to wave their prenuptial contract enticingly once more. 'Yes,' she agreed drearily.

Seth spent the afternoon clinching some deal, and Daisy took the bus back across the river to visit Jim and tell her mother that she was on her way to look for Tom at last. Their delight and gratitude was some comfort to her sore heart, but otherwise the trip was a ghastly reminder of how echoingly empty life was going to be without Seth. She looked around the house that she had grown up in and realised with a hollow certainty that it was no longer home. Home was in Seth's arms, and soon that would be gone too.

Seth had apparently forgotten that he was supposed to be showing her off as much as possible and took her instead to a small, quiet restaurant that evening. Both of them were subdued and both were equally determined not to show it, but their conversation kept sticking and then coming out in an awkward rush only to trail off into silence once more. Daisy didn't feel like eating much, anyway, and she was glad when Seth suggested that they left.

The hotel was so close that they walked back through the empty back streets—without touching, without talking. She mustn't waste this time with him, Daisy thought frantically as they took the lift together up to the top floor, but the realisation of how much she loved him had left her shy and tongue-tied and she didn't know how to make the first move. In the end it was Seth who made it. As he closed the door of the suite behind them the memory of how they had fallen in here yesterday, kissing and laughing breathlessly with desire, strummed unavoidably between them.

Seth looked at Daisy, who was standing uncertainly just inside the door. 'Have you changed your mind since yesterday?' he asked softly.

The tension left Daisy's shoulders. 'No,' she said, knowing only that she loved him and that tonight, of all nights, she needed the reassurance of his body. 'Have you?'

'No,' said Seth, and held out his hand. Daisy took it, and felt his fingers close around hers in an infinitely comforting clasp as he led her through to his room and made love to her with an intensity that left her awed and shaken.

Afterwards she lay beside him and watched him as he slept. The forbidding lines of his face relaxed in sleep and he looked younger and more vulnerable than she had ever seen him. Daisy remembered what Victoria had said about him needing someone to love him, and wished desperately that she could be that someone. She could wrap him in the security of her loving and protect him from the past and the present.

Only she wouldn't get the chance, she reminded herself sadly. Seth's vulnerability was just an illusion. He didn't need her or anyone else. 'I don't believe in love,' he had said. She had known all along that there was no point in falling in love with him and yet she had, and she couldn't find it in herself to regret it. She had made her choice: a few short weeks with Seth to balance against a whole lifetime without him—when this moment, lying next to him and resting her hand against his sleeping body, would be no more than a precious memory.

Daisy snuggled closer and began to tease Seth out of sleep with soft kisses. If memories were going to be all she would have left she would just have to ensure that they were happy ones...and that there were lots of them.

CHAPTER EIGHT

DAISY never forgot her first sight of Cutlass Cay. The afternoon glare had faded from the sky, leaving in its place a sort of hushed light that turned the sea to a shimmer of silver, as the seaplane dropped lower and lower.

The island itself was shaped like a teardrop and covered in a tangle of glossy green vegetation that sloped down from a jagged *piton* in its centre to a fringe of white sand. Curving in as the island narrowed was a small, sheltered bay, protected from the sea by a coral reef. A wooden jetty projected into the lagoon and behind it a long, low house was set back from the beach, its red corrugated iron roof half-hidden beneath luxuriant palms and a scramble of bougainvillea.

'What do you think?' asked Seth later, watching Daisy's face as she stood at the verandah rail and looked out at the leaning coconut palms that were silhouetted against a fiery sunset. The air was rich with the hot, lush, exotic smell of the Tropics and she could hear the sea breaking out on the reef.

'It's...beautiful,' she said, conscious of how inadequate it sounded, but it seemed to satisfy Seth.

'I'm glad you like it,' he said, as if it really mattered.

The house was cool and stylishly simple inside. Everything had been designed with immaculate taste but there was no stamp of Seth's personality anywhere, not even in the master bedroom with its pale, uncluttered walls and polished wooden floor. The vast mahogany bed was hung with a white gauze mosquito net which gave the room an airy, dream-like quality, but Daisy would have been more reassured to see a cluster of photographs or some well-thumbed books to disturb the cool elegance.

It reminded her all too clearly that Seth was a man who rejected the messiness of ties and commitments and emotional clutter. The room looked much more comfortable by the time she had spread her own mess around a bit, she decided, but she didn't think that Seth would agree.

If he noticed he didn't comment when they went to bed. Daisy was so tired from the long journey that she fell asleep almost as soon as she had crawled beneath the mosquito net and she didn't wake until late the next morning. Exotic-sounding birds were screeching in the undergrowth outside and the sea was murmuring invitingly onto the sand, but Daisy didn't want to move. The sun was striping through the shutters and throwing golden lines across the bed and Seth's lips were tantalising against her breast, and there was nowhere she wanted to be but here in this cool, wide bed she had eyed with such disfavour last night.

Stretching luxuriously, she turned into his arms with a sleepy smile and he lifted his head from her breast to look down into her face. Daisy had never imagined that his face could look so soft, his eyes so warm. 'Did I wake you?'

'I can't think of a nicer way to be woken up,' she said, drifting her hands up the powerfully muscled arms to his shoulders, and when he bent to kiss her the sun and the sea and the lushly beckoning beauty outside the window were all forgotten.

Later they walked hand in hand down to the white curving beach and sank into the lagoon. The water closed warm and silky around Daisy and she floated on her back, turning her face up to the sun. She had seen pictures of the Caribbean, of course, but she hadn't dreamed that the sea would really be this blue, the air this sparkling.

Seth's love-making was still tingling along her veins and she was so relaxed and replete that she didn't notice Seth dive beneath her until he grabbed her waist and pulled her down into the clear blue water. They surfaced together, Daisy spluttering in pretended indignation. Seth flicked his wet hair out of his eyes, and she saw him with a sudden, heart-clenching clarity—the drops of water on his lashes and on the sleek, brown shoulder, the lines starring his eyes, the very texture of his skin. The lagoon rocking around them threw wavering reflections over his face, and his teeth looked very white as he trod water and laughed down at her.

A happiness so intense that it hurt clutched at Daisy's heart. I'll never forget this moment, she realised fiercely. Whatever happens I'll remember how it is now with just the two of us, alone with the sea and the sunlight, and she put her arms around his neck and kissed him almost fiercely so that he wouldn't be able to read her expression.

They had breakfast on the verandah, watching the brightly coloured birds chattering and darting in and out of the greenery. Their activity only emphasised the utter peace of the scene, framed by the fringed palm trees, where there was only white sand and turquoise sea that stretched glittering, out to the horizon. 'I'd better go and make some calls,' Seth decided reluctantly at last. 'Maria will be wondering what's happened to me. I've usually checked in long before now.' He ran a careless finger down Daisy's cheek as he stood up. 'Don't get burnt.'

When he had gone Daisy sat for a while, treasuring the feel of his casual caress, then shook herself back to reality. Finding Tom was her priority, she reminded herself, not sitting here, intoxicated with happiness. With an effort she went to find the photograph of Tom she had brought with her.

The clearest one of him she had been able to find had been of the two of them together. Tom had his arm around her shoulder and they were smiling affectionately at each other. If Tom really *had* resented her mother marrying his father he had certainly never taken it out on Daisy. Both only children, they had immediately formed an alliance and treated each other as if they really had been brother and sister.

Daisy looked down at Tom's smiling face and sighed. 'Where am I going to find you, Tom?' she asked the photograph. She had been hoping that once she reached the Caribbean everything would fall in place, but it didn't look as if it was going to be that easy. One thing was for certain—he wasn't going to be on Cutlass Cay. She had to find someone who knew where a young Englishman might be working.

She decided to talk to the housekeeper first. She had only met Grace briefly last night, but the older woman had seemed calm and kind. Daisy found her in the guest quarters in the garden at the back of the house. Individual buildings, each with a sitting area and bathroom as well as a luxuriously appointed bedroom, were linked by wooden walkways so that although Seth's guests could have privacy when they wanted it there was still a feeling that they were all a part of the house.

Grace looked surprised to hear that Daisy wanted to ask her advice but readily walked back to the main house with her, leaving the two girls who were cleaning the rooms with a stern warning to carry on working.

'I don't rightly know what to suggest,' she admitted

when Daisy had explained that she wanted to trace someone. 'You'd be best to ask Mr Seth.'

'As me what?' said Seth's voice behind them.

'How to trace someone,' said Daisy a little awkwardly, and Grace automatically handed him the photograph.

'Winston would know how to find him, wouldn't he?' she said to Seth. 'He knows everybody.'

'Is this man the reason you were so anxious to come to the Caribbean?' Seth asked Daisy.

'Yes,' she admitted, glad to be able to tell him at last. 'I've got to find him as soon as I can. You see—' She broke off as Seth held up a hand.

'If you want to find him that badly then of course I'll put one of my men onto it,' he said in a colourless voice. 'What's his name?'

'Tom. Tom Johnson.'

Seth looked down again at the photograph of Tom with his arm around Daisy and his face became shuttered, but all he said was, 'It would help if I could keep this picture.'

'Of course,' said Daisy gratefully. It had only been borne on her this morning what an impossible task she had set herself, and it felt as if a huge burden had been lifted off her shoulders to know that Seth would delegate someone far more capable than her to find Tom. Why hadn't she asked Seth before? 'The last I heard he was in the Bahamas but that was nearly a year ago, and he might be anywhere by now.'

'If he's in the Caribbean Winston will find him for you,' said Seth flatly. 'I'll get him onto it right away.'

He had turned back into his office before Daisy had a chance to explain who Tom was, but she told herself that she could make their relationship clearer to Seth later when she thanked him.

But Seth, when he found her later—lying on a lounger under the coconut palms—refused to be thanked and wouldn't listen to any explanations. Daisy's eyes were closed, a contented smile just curling her mouth, and she didn't hear him approaching on the soft sand. It wasn't until he placed a hand on either arm of the lounger and bent to kiss her lips that her eyes flew open.

'Seth!' Smiling, she relaxed back into the cushions. 'You startled me!'

'You were miles away.' He hesitated. 'Dreaming about Tom Johnson?'

'No,' Daisy began, but Seth interrupted her almost roughly.

'You needn't worry. Winston's organising a trace right away.'

'I don't know how to thank you,' she said sincerely, putting out a hand, and he closed his fingers around it so tightly that she winced.

'I don't want your thanks,' he said in a harsh voice. 'You can think of Winston's services as part of the deal.'

'But, Seth, if I could just explain about Tom—'

'No!' he said fiercely. 'I don't want to hear any explanations, Daisy. What you do when you leave here is your business. That's what we agreed.'

'I know, but—'

'But nothing. I don't want to know what you're going to do, or who you're going to do it with. What we have now is a temporary thing—we both know that. Astra is coming out in a couple of weeks, and then we'll go our separate ways. That was the deal, wasn't it?'

'Yes,' said Daisy, looking blindly out to sea as she thought about Astra. That *was* the deal.

Seth lifted her hand to his mouth and kissed her palm, then her wrist and then the soft skin of her inner arm. 'That was the deal,' he repeated. 'And then we made

another deal—not to think about the future at all. Just
for now we're here together, Daisy. Let's not spoil it by
having to explain anything.' His lips had reached her
elbow, and were tracing a shivery path up to her shoulder.

'All right,' said Daisy, touching his hair with her free
hand. 'If that's what you want.'

Seth was right, she told herself later. It was silly to
waste the time they had—the present was all that mattered.

The next few days were idyllic. Refusing to think about
the future, Daisy spent her time swinging indolently in
a hammock. Sometimes she would rouse herself to wade
into the sparkling turquoise water or walk through the
wonderful, wild gardens which merged inextricably with
the rain forest, but mostly she was content to wait for
Seth to come out and join her.

He was in touch with his headquarters every day, but
was spending less and less time on the phone. Daisy
tried to tell herself not to get used to having him around,
but she couldn't help the way everything took on a new
intensity when he was there. All he had to do was sit
beside her and suddenly the world was brighter and more
brilliant than before. She would be piercingly aware of
the sunlight spangling the lagoon, the fringed shadows
of the palms on the white sand, the bright scarlet
splashes of hibiscus and the sudden squawk and flash of
a parrot's wing.

In the evenings they would watch the sunset in the
fading light, and the feel of her fingers curled around
the coolness of a glass would be enough to send a shiver
of pure joy down her spine. One of the shy girls would
serve them dinner at the polished mahogany dining-table
while the old-fashioned ceiling fan circled lazily above

them, and afterwards they would walk barefoot along the beach in the velvety darkness—where the only sound was the frantic whirring of the insects in the trees and the soft, rippling sigh of the wavelets in the lagoon on the sand. And then they would slide beneath the mosquito net onto the cool bed, and nothing would exist but the feel of Seth's body and the touch of his hands and the hammering pleasure they discovered together.

Nearly a week had passed in a haze of happiness when Daisy went in search of Grace once more, but this time it was only for a vase. Seth was in his office and she had spent a happy hour, gathering flowers in the gardens. Her arms full of vivid blooms, she found Grace in the huge, welcoming kitchen. 'I'm a florist,' she explained when the housekeeper lifted her brows in astonishment at her request for a vase. 'The flowers were so beautiful that I couldn't resist them.'

Grace continued with her preparations for the evening meal and watched Daisy's absorbed face under her lashes as she sorted out the blooms with deft fingers. 'Is Mr Seth in his office?'

'He had to check some message on his computer,' said Daisy vaguely, stripping the greenery off the lower stalks. 'He said he wouldn't be long.'

'Seems like he hasn't spent much time in there this visit,' commented Grace mildly, without looking up from her chopping. 'He's more relaxed than I've ever seen him.'

'How could anyone not be relaxed in such a beautiful place?' she asked with a happy sigh.

'It's not usually a rest for Mr Seth when he comes. He'll bring a dozen guests with him and even then he'll spend half the day in his office.' Grace shot Daisy a quick, bright glance. 'He's different this time. I've known him since he was a boy, and I ain't never seen

him like this before. Seems like he's really enjoying
himself for the first time.'

Daisy's face was soft. 'I hope so,' she said, arranging
the stems carefully in the vase. 'I didn't realise you'd
been here so long, Grace. Doesn't it get boring here on
your own? Seth doesn't come here that often does he?'

'About three times a year, that's all, but the house
isn't often empty. When Mr Seth's not here he lets people who work for him come down. Not just executives,
either,' confided Grace. 'Anyone who comes to his attention—he'll send them down here for a holiday. It
don't matter whether they wash his cars or run one of
his companies, we look after them just the same as we
do him.'

'He didn't tell me that,' said Daisy slowly, staring at
a branch of bougainvillea for a moment before sliding it
into the vase.

'Mr Seth's not one to boast about what he does—not
like some,' said Grace with an audible sniff. 'Not like
that Astra Bentingger, for instance. She makes sure
everyone knows how much she gives to charity, but I
ain't never seen her give anyone a kind word. Mr Seth,
he's got a reputation as a hard man, but I ain't never
heard anyone who works for him complain. When
Winston's little son was ill Mr Seth heard about it somehow, and he flew him straight away to the States and
paid for all his medical treatment. You won't hear
Winston say a word against him, that's for sure.'

Daisy continued to arrange the flowers automatically,
but her expression was thoughtful. This was a new side
to Seth. There had been times over the last few days
when she'd been sure that she knew everything important that there was to know about him, but it seemed that
wasn't so. 'Who is Winston, Grace?' she asked, remembering suddenly where she had heard the name before.

It was Winston who had been given the task of tracing Tom.

'Winston? I'm not sure what you'd call him, but he does whatever needs doing round here. I don't know what he does when he's not here, but he knows everybody.' Grace kept her voice neutral, but her eyes were alive with curiosity. 'You heard anything about your missing friend yet?'

Daisy shook her head. 'Tom isn't my friend,' she said, suddenly desperate to tell someone. 'He's my stepbrother. He had a terrible row with my stepfather and left home about eighteen months ago. He hasn't been in touch since then, but we heard he was working in the Caribbean. Jim—that's my stepfather—was furious with him at first, but now he's very ill and he's desperate to see Tom again before he dies.' She sighed and worry clouded her eyes. A brief phone call home to her mother had reassured her that Jim was still holding his own, but how long could he continue to live on hope?

'I tried explaining to Seth,' Daisy went on, concentrating deliberately on the final touches to the arrangement, 'but…well, he doesn't really care who Tom is.'

'Doesn't care?' Grace said incredulously, her knife freezing in mid-chop.

Daisy flushed. 'Yes. We…that is…this is just a temporary thing for both of us,' she found herself explaining with a tinge of desperation.

'Hmm.' Grace's snort was eloquent in its disbelief but, to Daisy's relief, she changed the subject, nodding instead at the sea framed by the kitchen window. 'Going to be a storm tonight,' she predicted darkly.

Sure enough, outside the clouds were already boiling moodily on the horizon. It was very hot, and the afternoon took on an almost eerie stillness as they approached. The storm itself didn't hit the island until five o'clock. The birds fell uncannily silent and the palms began to sway in the hot wind, and then abruptly the storm was upon them. Daisy was unprepared for its ferocity. The rain thundered on the corrugated iron roof and the whole house seemed to creak and rattle before the screaming wind. It raged at the storm shutters that Grace had lowered around the verandah, whipping the trees into a frenzy in its frustration.

Daisy was gripped by a queer mixture of fear and excitement, and she shifted closer to Seth. 'Can I hold your hand?' she asked, only half joking.

His clasp was warm and strong and infinitely comforting. 'I used to love the storms here when I was a boy,' he told her. 'They were so wild and uncontrollable. When the electricity went off, like now, I'd sit out here in the dark on my own and listen to the wind and pretend I was marooned, like Robinson Crusoe.'

'It must have been lovely to be able to come here whenever you wanted,' said Daisy wistfully, thinking of the time when she would have to leave—never to come back.

'Neither of my parents liked it that much.' It was already so dark that Grace had lit a hurricane lamp. It hissed on the table beside them, throwing bizarre, flickering shadows against the storm shutters.

'They must have done!' she protested, unable to conceive of anyone not liking this beautiful island. 'Why else would they buy it?'

'It was my grandfather who bought Cutlass Cay,' Seth said. 'He'd worked his way up from nothing—the proverbial rags-to-riches story—and for him this island represented everything he'd ever dreamed about. But my parents took it for granted. They'd always had so much that they never knew how lucky they were. For them, Cutlass Cay was just a status symbol—something to boast about.' His eyes rested on the uneasy shadows. 'If they'd had an even worse argument than usual one of them might bring me down here and play at being alone for a day or so, but it wasn't long before they'd start to pine for civilisation and I'd get dragged off somewhere else. I never knew where I was going to be the next day.'

His voice was quite expressionless, but Daisy had a sudden glimpse of a confused little boy left to sit on his own during a storm. During her own childhood she had often grumbled about the predictability of the home routine, but at least she had had a home. Perhaps being able to play Robinson Crusoe on your very own desert island hadn't been that much fun after all.

'It must have been very unsettling,' she said quietly.

Seth shrugged. 'I learnt that it was easier not to rely on anyone else, that's all. It's hard to make friends when you're constantly being whisked from one place to another without warning, so I got used to being on my own. Children accept things like that. I suppose I thought that everybody's mother spent all morning in bed and only got up to go out again.'

'Who looked after you?'

'Oh…a succession of nannies. They never lasted very long. Most of them ended up having an affair with my father, and then leaving in tears when my mother decided to restake her claim on him.' Seth's lips twisted in a rueful smile. 'I can remember being almost relieved when they finally got divorced. I was only eight, and they used to use me for scoring points off each other. 'I thought that, perhaps, if they were going to live apart life might settle down.'

His face was bleak with memory. Daisy tightened her hand around his, but she didn't say anything. He had never opened up about his family before, and she didn't want to interrupt him. After a while he went on, 'My mother swept in one day and told me that she was taking me away to live with her for good. I was thrilled, of course—you know what little boys are like about their mothers.'

'What was she like?' Daisy asked softly.

'She was very beautiful,' said Seth. 'Beautiful and dazzling and utterly heartless, and I adored her. Sometimes it suited her to play the affectionate mother, usually in front of an audience, and she would be all over me, but it irritated her that I wanted attention. I was supposed to just sit and look adoring until one of her lovers arrived, at which point I was told to go away. When she and my father were divorced I stayed with her for about six weeks before she decided that I was in the way and sent me back to my father.

'After that I got used to shuttling between them whenever a new partner appeared on the scene. I'd had three stepmothers and four stepfathers by the time I left school, and those were only the official ones.' He glanced suddenly at Daisy. 'You can see why I ended up with a rather jaundiced view of marriage.'

'I'm beginning to,' she said in a low voice, conscious of a blind hatred of the parents who had treated a little boy's love with such callous indifference. No wonder Seth had grown up into a hard man!

'I was always surprised that they kept on getting married,' Seth went on after a while. 'You'd have thought that experience would have taught them that it wasn't worth the bother, but they never seemed to realise that they were just using other people—and being used in return. All the women I ever met used to spend their time talking about love, but all they really wanted was novelty. A new lover didn't mean much more than a new dress or a new car but once they got married things immediately got messy, and all those marriages that started off with extravagant vows of love ended up as a sordid bickering over money.'

Daisy watched the hissing lamp. 'It doesn't have to be like that,' she said quietly, understanding at last why he had insisted on that cold-blooded contract with Astra. He was only looking reality in the face.

'No,' said Seth bleakly. 'But it usually is, isn't it?'

He was still holding her hand, but Daisy sensed his withdrawal. 'Seth might have had a lot of lovers but I don't think he's ever had much loving.' Victoria's words seemed to echo in the dark verandah as the wind shrieked and the rain thundered on the roof, and abruptly Daisy made up her mind. There was no point in arguing with Seth or trying to change his mind. It was too late for that now. All she could do was give him some of the loving he had missed out on while she could.

Seth's expression hardened as Daisy released his hand and stood up, but when she put her hands wordlessly around his neck and slid onto his lap his whole body seemed to relax and his arms came round her. 'Let's not talk about marriage,' she murmured, kissing his ear. 'Let's talk about being alone in the dark with the storm outside.'

'Let's not talk at all,' said Seth, and found her mouth with his own.

The electric atmosphere of the storm gave their love-making a new urgency and excitement that night. Outside the wind screamed and shook the shutters and the rain continued to pound on the corrugated iron roof, but a different elemental force had Seth and Daisy in its power. The drumming of the rain was no more than a faint echo of the drumming desire that beat its insistent rhythm between them, and the strength of the winds was as nothing to the turbulent passion that lifted them, spun them round and bore them up and up to a different plane.

Much later Daisy lay and listened to Seth breathing beside her and realised that the storm had blown itself out. The winds had dropped as abruptly as they had arisen, and all that was left of the downpour was the slow drip from the banana leaves outside the window. It sounded as if the island was as hushed and replete as she felt herself.

The air was crystalline the next morning, as if the rain had washed everything clean and left the island diamond bright. Only the battered foliage, still damp and steaming gently in the heat, gave any sign of the previous night's storm.

'I should show you more of the island,' Seth said to Daisy over breakfast. 'Let's go and explore some of the beaches on the other side.'

Daisy's face lit up at the thought of spending the whole day with him, but then she hesitated. 'Don't you have to ring Maria?'

'She can send a fax if there are any urgent messages,' he said. 'If I ring her now there's bound to be something that needs to be dealt with, and I'll be in there all morning.'

'What if there's some kind of crisis?'

'It can wait,' said Seth.

Grace prepared them a picnic and they took the speed-boat. It skimmed over the glittering waves, and Daisy felt exhilaration bubbling along her veins like champagne at the combination of speed and Seth and the sun reflected on the blue, blue sea. The sheer sides of the volcanic *piton* dropped dramatically down to the sea, making the beaches on the far side of the island accessible only by boat, and the sand was so smooth that it

was easy to imagine that no one had ever been there
before them.

Seth cut the engine and they jumped out to splash
through the shallows and drag the boat up onto the
beach. They had planned to circumnavigate the island,
exploring all the beaches, but somehow they never got
beyond the first. It was too comfortable, lying in the
shade of the palms and savouring the utter tranquillity.
Every now and then a bird cried raucously from the forest, but otherwise the only sounds were the tiny ripples
breaking onto the sand and the occasional cat's-paw of
breeze just riffling the surface of the sea and stirring the
leaves above them so that the shadows swayed over their
skin.

'It's so peaceful,' sighed Daisy contentedly, turning
onto her stomach and propping herself up on her elbows.

'Mmm,' said Seth lazily, without opening his eyes. 'I
should do this more often. No crises to deal with; no
deal to be made; no reception to attend...'

'No one to impress and absolutely nothing to do,' she
agreed with another blissful sigh.

There was a pause, then Seth opened one eye. Daisy
was lying close beside him. The wind on the boat had
left her soft curls even more tousled than usual but the
sun had given her skin a golden bloom and the dark blue
eyes, so like the colour of the sea beyond the reef, were
aglow with happiness. He ran his hand up her side.
'There is *one* thing we could do,' he said speculatively.

Daisy tried to prim her mouth but her eyes danced.
'Why, Mr Carrington, what *are* you suggesting?'

'I wouldn't want you getting bored,' Seth explained,
continuing to trace a feather-light pattern of desire on
her warm golden skin.

Smiling, she leant over him, but as she looked down
into his face her smile faded. 'I've never felt less bored,'

she said, as if she had to convince him of something vital. Slowly, very slowly, she lowered her mouth to his, and Seth's hands came up to pull her down on top of him for a kiss that went on and deliciously on. Daisy felt herself dissolving at the hard demand of his body as they gave themselves up to the timeless spin of desire, and the glitteringly bright world outside this small patch of shade was forgotten until an outraged squawk from the undergrowth shattered the peace. The next instant two parrots had erupted out of the trees in a blur of yellow and green.

'I think we're shocking the parrots,' Daisy murmured against Seth's lips, and he laughed and rolled her beneath him.

'They can look the other way if they don't like it,' he said.

The sky had lost its glare and the sun had begun its slow descent to the horizon by the time they pushed the boat out from the beach at last and headed reluctantly back to the house. Tying up expertly at the jetty, Seth helped Daisy out. She smiled up at him as he steadied her, and his fingers tightened convulsively around her arms.

'Daisy,' he said with sudden urgency and, at the look in his eyes, the breath leaked out of her lungs.

'Yes?'

'Daisy, I— But Seth got no further. A voice was calling his name imperatively from the verandah and they both jerked round to see a stunningly beautiful woman coming down the steps towards the jetty, her arms open wide. Daisy wouldn't have needed to have seen her pictures in a thousand magazines to know at once who she was and why she was there.

It was Astra, and she had come for Seth.

CHAPTER NINE

'THERE you are, darling!' Astra's voice was low, mellifluous and utterly confident of her welcome.

'Astra?' Seth sounded as jarred and disorientated as Daisy felt. His hands dropped slowly from her arms. 'What are you doing here?'

'I thought I'd surprise you,' laughed Astra, kissing him full on the mouth, and Daisy's hands clenched into fists so tight that her fingernails dug into her palms. 'I know we decided it would be better if we weren't seen together, but I couldn't stay away any longer.' She sent Seth an arch look under her impossibly long lashes. 'You needn't look so worried, darling! I was careful to bring a select group of friends with me as "cover"!'

'Why didn't you let me know you were coming?' Daisy took some comfort from the fact that Seth hadn't actually swept Astra into his arms…but, then, why would he? He had never pretended to be madly in love with her, but it didn't mean that he didn't still want to marry her.

'I rang you this morning,' said Astra, as if a few hours' notice was more than adequate. 'Apparently, you'd just left so I told your housekeeper to make sure all the guest quarters were ready.' Her voice thinned slightly. 'You might have a word with her, Seth. I have to say that her manner wasn't at *all* welcoming. I actually had to remind her who I was!'

Before Seth could reply Astra had turned her dazzling smile on Daisy. 'And you must be Daisy!' she said, with just a hint of condescension. 'I can't tell you how grateful I am—Seth has told me all about what a *marvellous* job you've been doing. We must have a lovely chat later on.' She tucked her hand proprietorially through Seth's arm. 'Come on in and meet the others, darling. They've all been wondering what's happened to you, and I don't want it to look as if I'm hogging you to myself!'

Seth's face was a mask as Astra swept him up to the verandah with her. Daisy was left to trail behind them. She felt sick. She wanted to scream and shout and snatch Astra's hand away from Seth, but of course she couldn't. She had known all along that it would end like this. Perhaps it was better after all not to have had any warning. It meant that there was no temptation to break their agreement and tell Seth how much she loved him after all.

Daisy was furious with herself for succumbing to the heedless enchantment of the last week. It had been so easy to think that she would be able to walk away when the time came. Why hadn't she realised how agonising it would be to say goodbye and face up to a life without him?

She couldn't even blame Seth. As if from a great distance, Daisy watched him greeting the gaggle of people draped languidly around the living-room. He had recovered his countenance and was being the charming host—smiling, chatting easily, apologising for his absence. This was the suave, coolly assured tycoon she had first met; the man she had fallen more and more deeply in love with over the last few days had vanished so utterly that he might never have been.

A cold feeling of bitter inevitability closed around Daisy's heart and she turned away, muttering something about getting changed. She longed for Seth to make a similar excuse and join her in the bedroom so that they could at least talk, but he didn't. Dully, Daisy showered and dressed alone. What had she expected? that he would turn his back on his whole life and choose her over Astra?

The pictures she had seen hadn't prepared Daisy for Astra's incandescent beauty or the effortless way she carried everyone before her. She was the perfect partner for a man like Seth, Daisy realised miserably. How could she think that the past week would count for anything, compared to what Astra offered him—wealth, intelligence, beauty, an instinctive understanding of the pressures of his business life?

It wasn't as if Seth hadn't made his position absolutely clear. He had never said that he loved her; had never promised anything that he wasn't able to give. When he touched her, when he smiled at her, it hadn't seemed as if any words were necessary, but now the words *I love you* mocked Daisy with their absence. Not once had Seth let slip anything that she might use to comfort herself now.

Daisy thought about the day they had just spent with something like pain. Could it really have meant nothing to Seth? Could he really not have felt the magic of those long hours in the shade? When he had helped her out of the boat onto the jetty she had been so sure that he was going to tell her that he loved her then...but he hadn't. If he had wanted to he could have come to tell her now...but he hadn't.

She would just have to accept that.

Astra was waiting for her when she came out of the room. 'I wanted to catch you on your own,' the American said with a smile that didn't quite reach her eyes. 'Seth's gone off to call his office, and I thought it would be a good opportunity for us to have a chat—just the two of us.'

She made it sound as if she and Daisy were bosom

friends, dying for a girlish gossip. The last thing Daisy
wanted was to talk to anyone, least of all Astra, but the
news that Seth had had plenty of opportunity to come
and see her and had chosen to go to his study instead
sent a warming flicker of pride and anger along her veins
and, instead of making some excuse, she agreed to the
idea coolly.

'Marvellous!' said Astra, although it was doubtful if
it had even occurred to her that Daisy might refuse. It
was hard to imagine anyone ever refusing Astra anything. 'Let's go to my bungalow.' She led the way along
one of the exterior walkways that joined the guest quarters to the main house. 'I'm sleeping out here, for ap-
pearances' sake,' she informed Daisy with another show
of girlish confidence. 'Seth can slip along later tonight
when we've both put on a show of going to separate
rooms. Ridiculous, isn't it?' she added with a world-
weary laugh. 'But Dimitrios is madly suspicious, as it
is. We can't be too careful at this stage.'

Each of the guest bungalows had a small, private verandah. Unperturbed by Daisy's lack of response, Astra
waved her regally towards one of the comfortable wicker
chairs and sank into the other with an exaggerated sigh.
'I can't tell you how nice it is to be able to talk to
someone who knows the truth. It's been ghastly trying
to pretend that Seth means nothing to me!'

Sheer hatred held Daisy's throat in a tight grip, making it hard to speak. 'What did you want to talk to me
about?' she managed at last in a tight, hard, little voice.

'I just wanted to *thank* you.' Astra leant forward, vi-
brant, lovely, the perfect friend. 'Really, Daisy, you've
been fantastic. You've certainly managed to convince
everyone that you and Seth are an item, and it's taken
all the speculation off me. I can't tell you how much we
both appreciate it.'

Her tone was warm and sincere, but the warning in the beautiful green eyes was unmistakable. Astra had seen that little scene on the jetty and had decided to remind Daisy just what she was there for. So Daisy decided, anyway.

'I was just doing what I'm being paid to do,' she said flatly.

'I must admit that Seth told me that you weren't a very good actress at first,' Astra confided with another little laugh, 'but you've proved him wrong. You managed to fool Stephen Rickman, anyway, and not many people do that!'

Daisy looked wary. 'What do you mean?'

'He wrote the most extraordinary article about Seth,' said Astra, a little too casually. 'All about how Seth was a changed man.' Picking up a newspaper cutting from the table beside her, she read aloud.

'Carrington seems to have found a meaning and a purpose in life at last... Those who have reason to fear him as a ruthless business operator would be hard put to recognise the man smiling down at the girl he so clearly loves... Daisy Deare has a quality of shining innocence rare in the world of men like Seth Carrington... The bond between them obviously goes far beyond the almost tangible sexual tension... Seeing the warmth in Daisy Deare's captivating blue eyes, it is hard not to envy Carrington—not for the power he wields or the family fortune that he has restored so dramatically, but because he is a man who has, against all the odds, found the other half of himself.'

Astra broke off. 'Well, it goes on and on,' she said dismissively. 'Rickman was obviously very taken with you!' She tossed the cutting across to Daisy. 'Rather a touching picture too.'

The photographer had caught Seth and Daisy laughing

into each other's eyes, oblivious to the camera. In silence
Daisy stared down at it then picked it up, her heart twisting painfully. She remembered that moment. She remembered every time that Seth had smiled at her; every
time he had touched her. No one seeing that picture
would believe that they weren't two people deeply in
love. Only she knew that on this occasion the camera
had, indeed, lied.

She handed the cutting back to Astra. 'It's lucky that
Seth is such a good actor, too, isn't it?'

'Very lucky,' Astra agreed, but her eyes were cold.

'You must be pleased,' Daisy persevered.

For a second Astra looked taken aback. 'Pleased?'

'I thought this was exactly the kind of publicity you
wanted?'

'Oh, it is. The article's been syndicated all round the
world. I didn't see it until yesterday.'

She must have been pretty worried if she had dropped
everything and flown straight out to the Caribbean,
Daisy reflected with bleak humour. Perhaps Astra wasn't
quite as sure of Seth as she pretended to be. Suddenly
she was fed up with playing games.

'Did you come to find out whether it was true or not?'

Astra clearly didn't like the initiative being taken out
of her own capable hands, but she recovered quickly.
'Oh, I wasn't worried about Seth but I was a *teeny* bit
worried about *you*, I have to admit. Seth's a very attractive man—no one knows that better than I do—and if
you were spending all day and all night with him...well,
I wouldn't have wanted you to get hurt.'

'What about the possibility of Seth being the one to
get hurt?'

'Oh, I wasn't worried about that.' Astra's confidence
set Daisy's teeth on edge. 'You see, Daisy, I *know* Seth.
We come from similar backgrounds and we understand

each other. He can't bear messy, emotional affairs. As soon as he thinks a girl is getting too involved he gets rid of her as fast as he can. He doesn't want that kind of commitment. When we're married he knows I won't cling around his neck or expect him to spend all day making love to me,' she added complacently. 'I've got my own companies to run.'

It was only what Seth himself had said. Why did it hurt so much to hear it from Astra as well? Daisy made a great effort to steady her voice. 'You needn't worry,' she said. 'I've got no intention of clinging around Seth's neck.'

'I hoped you'd think like that.' Astra's green eyes rested on Daisy's face with satisfaction. 'I hope you realise that I've just got your best interests at heart, Daisy. I've told my lawyers to agree to Seth's final terms so we should be able to sign the pre-nuptial contract any day now. Once we've done that I'll be divorcing Dimitrios, and then Seth and I can get married.' She looked smugly round her. 'We'll probably spend our honeymoon here.'

The thought of Seth making love to Astra was a knife, twisting so savagely in Daisy's heart that she had to clench her jaw to stop herself from crying out in pain. Her voice seemed to be coming from a long way away. 'So you won't need me much longer?'

'I think Seth will agree that you've served your purpose,' said Astra. 'But you've done a marvellous job, and we're both so pleased that we felt you deserved a little bonus.'

'What sort of bonus?'

The American picked up a long, flat leather box from the table and handed it to Daisy with a patronising smile. 'Seth and I hope you'll accept this as a token of our appreciation.'

'*Seth and I*'? So they'd discussed her, had they? All the time that she had been stupidly hoping that Seth would join her in the bedroom he had been closeted with Astra, deciding how best to get rid of her! Daisy's misery was focusing into a cold, comforting centre of fury—with Astra's condescending attitude, with Seth for leaving it to his fiancée to give her the brush-off but most of all with herself for having had the presumption to hope that things might be different.

With a set face she opened the box. Inside, a diamond bracelet lay glittering on a bed of velvet and, in spite of herself, Daisy stared at it. Stones of that quality had to be worth a small fortune, certainly far more than the flower shop would earn in a year.

'We know that girls in your…er…*profession* distrust cheques,' Astra went on with a show of delicate hesitation.

Daisy looked up from the box. 'My profession?'

'My dear, we all know what sort of actress Dee Pearce is! Why do you think Seth approached her in the first place?' Astra examined her perfectly manicured nails. 'I'm not unreasonable. Seth's a man after all, and I wouldn't expect him to spend that much time with a girl without sleeping with her. Oh, don't bother to deny it!' she said as Daisy stiffened. 'I knew it as soon as I saw you standing together on the jetty. *I* don't mind. I know quite well that Seth's not a man likely to confuse love and sex. My only concern, as I said before, was to make sure that you hadn't.'

'*I'd better make sure I get my money's worth.*' Seth's words echoed jeeringly in Daisy's brain as she looked blindly back at the bracelet. Its sparkling beauty seemed to mock her dreams. *Sex*—was that really all that the last couple of weeks had meant to Seth?

Numbly she closed the leather box and stood up. 'You

can keep your bonus,' she said in a voice devoid
expression. 'All Seth needs to do is to pay me the money
we agreed, and then I'll go.' Dropping the box back into
Astra's lap, she turned and walked out without another
word.

Reaction set in almost immediately, and she began to
shake uncontrollably. Unable to face going back to the
house, she found a secluded seat where the gardens suc-
cumbed to the luxuriant chaos of the rain forest and sank
down onto it. Everything was just the same as it had
been since she'd arrived on Cutlass Cay.

The brightly coloured birds continued to squabble excitedly in the trees; the sea, glimpsed through a clearing
in the undergrowth, still stretched blue and glittering to
the horizon. The sun still shone, piercing the dark glossy
foliage with beams of light or throwing an eerie green
glow over the shade. The hibiscus still bloomed, the
bougainvillea still scrambled vividly along the verandahs
but, for Daisy, it was as if the world had been drained
of all colour. The brightness and the brilliance had faded
to a dreary monotone and the only feeling that existed
was the raw, raging pain inside her.

What a fool she had been! What a blind, besotted,
stupid little fool! She had let herself fall hopelessly in
love with Seth and all the time he had been thinking of
her as no more than a commodity—something he had
bought. Suddenly everything Seth had ever said or done
fell into place and Daisy saw her own position with hid-
eous, humiliating clarity. She had demeaned and de-
graded herself, and if Seth thought that she was merely
a thing to be used and discarded it was partly her own
fault.

Too desperate even to cry, Daisy sat as the evening
gathered around her—her fingers gripping the wooden
slats of the bench as if they were all that was holding

her together. Her face was so ravaged that the man crossing the grass towards her in the tropical dusk hesitated to intrude at first. 'Miss Daisy?' he said gently at last, and Daisy's eyes focused with an effort on a concerned face. 'Miss Daisy, are you all right?'

'Yes,' she said dully. 'I'm fine.'

'I'm Winston.' He hesitated again. 'Could I have a word with you a minute?'

Daisy made a desperate effort to pull herself together. 'Of course.' She moved stiffly along the bench to make room for him. 'Sit down.'

Winston sat, casting another worried look at the bleakness of her expression. 'It's just that I don't know what to do,' he explained. 'I've been waiting all day to speak to the boss, but now he's gone and shut himself in his study and says he doesn't want to be disturbed. I need to know what he wants me to do about that fellow he asked me to find for you.'

'Tom?' said Daisy with difficulty. 'You've found Tom?'

'We found him four days ago,' said Winston. 'I've been keeping an eye on him, like the boss said, but now he's got a boat from somewhere and is talking about moving on. He hasn't said where he's going, and I don't know whether the boss wants me to keep track of him or stop him leaving.'

His words sank slowly into Daisy's numb brain. 'You found Tom *four days* ago?' she repeated stupidly. 'Why didn't you tell us?'

'I did,' said Winston in surprise. 'I told the boss and he said just to make sure he didn't leave.'

'Do you mean that Seth has known where Tom is for the last four days?'

'Didn't he tell you?'

'No,' said Daisy grimly. 'He didn't tell me.' The fury

blazing through her scorched the raw nerve endings ⸤ misery but it warmed and invigorated her at the same time, and she was grateful. How dared Seth keep Tom's whereabouts a secret from her? How *dared* he? Daisy thought of her stepfather, lying patiently in hospital, and the bitter anger grew to a white-hot intensity. Tom could have been at Jim's bedside three days ago if it hadn't been for Seth Carrington!

Her eyes were a dark, dangerous blue as she got to her feet. 'Where is Tom now?'

'St Lucia.'

'Will you take me there tomorrow morning?'

Winston looked uneasy. 'I'd need to clear it with the boss.'

'I'll clear it with Seth,' said Daisy. 'I think you'll find that he'll be glad to be rid of me!'

Seth's study door was still closed as she marched back into the house. About to hammer on it, Daisy stopped and then dropped her arm. It would be better to phone her mother first so that she could pass the news on to Jim as soon as possible. There was a phone in the bedroom. She could use that. Seth was unlikely to come in there now that Astra was installed in her private bungalow, Daisy remembered bitterly.

'You know where Tom is?' Ellen said excitedly when Daisy told her what she knew. 'Oh, darling, that's wonderful news! How on earth did you find him?'

'It's rather a long story, Mum. I'll tell you when I get back. I just thought you'd want to know as soon as possible.'

'I'll go round and tell Jim right away,' her mother said. The relief in her voice rang down the phone line from the other side of the Atlantic. 'He was beginning to give up hope, I'm afraid, but this will make all the difference. When do you think you'll be able to come back?'

'I'm going to St Lucia first thing tomorrow morning and as soon as I've seen Tom I'll book the first flight home. With any luck, we'll be back in a couple of days.'

A note of doubt crept into Ellen's tone. 'What if Tom won't listen to you?'

'He will,' said Daisy confidently. 'You know how close Tom and I have always been. He'll come back for me, I'm sure of it.'

Without warning, the sound of the door being snapped closed made Daisy's heart jerk alarmingly and she spun round. Seth was standing just inside the room, and the look on his face sent the blood racing frantically along her veins. Across the room their eyes met with a such jarring impact that Daisy half expected to see sparks flying through the air.

'I've got to go,' she said slowly into the receiver, but without taking her gaze from Seth. 'I'll let you know exactly when we're coming back as soon as I can.'

Very carefully, she put the phone down.

'What was all that about?' demanded Seth in a savage voice.

Daisy walked across to the wardrobe and pulled down her case. 'I'm going home.'

'What do you mean, you're going home?'

'Just that,' said Daisy, passionately grateful for the anger that burned hard and bright inside her. 'I'm leaving here with Winston first thing tomorrow morning.'

'You're not going anywhere,' said Seth harshly. 'We had an agreement, in case you'd forgotten.'

'I haven't forgotten.' Bleakness swept across Daisy's face, but her back was turned to him and he didn't see. 'I've kept my part, and now I'd like my money so that I can go.'

'Go where? To Tom?' He turned the name into a sneer and Daisy swung round, incandescent with rage.

'Yes, to Tom!' she repeated. 'I've just had a very illuminating little chat with Winston. You knew perfectly well how much I wanted to find Tom. You've known where he was for *four* days, and you deliberately kept it secret from me!'

'Why should I tell you?' Seth countered callously. 'I wasn't having you running off to join your lover before I'd finished with you.'

Daisy was too angry to correct him about Tom. Let him think that Tom was her lover! 'Well, I understand that you've ''finished with'' me now!'

Seth had taken a step towards her but he stopped abruptly. 'What do you mean?'

'Astra informs me that I've done such a good job that my services aren't required any more. The bonus was a nice idea but, frankly, I'd rather have the cash!'

'I don't know anything about a bonus, but I know that you're not getting any money from me until you've done what you came out to do!'

'I've already done that,' said Daisy coldly. 'I came out to find Tom, and now that I've found him I don't have to spend any longer with an arrogant, manipulative bastard!'

'*Manipulative*? You dare call *me* manipulative?' Seth was very white about the mouth. 'How else would you describe *your* performance over the last few days?'

'As just that—a performance.' The white heat of anger was leaving Daisy unnaturally cold and controlled. 'You don't really think I'd have put up with you if I wasn't being paid for it, do you?'

The expression in Seth's eyes made her take a hasty step backwards, but he didn't touch her. 'You haven't been paid yet,' he reminded her unpleasantly. 'You

won't get very far without money or your passport,
which I've still got, and—unless you're planning to
swim—you're stuck here until I say you can go, so
you'd better start performing again pretty damn quick!'

'Winston's got a boat.'

Seth folded his arms. 'Winston won't take you anywhere without my approval.'

Frustrated, Daisy glared at him. 'What's the point in
making me stay?' she demanded. 'You don't need me
any more.'

'I'll be the judge of that.'

'But you can't keep me a prisoner here!'

'I think you'll find that I can do whatever I want,'
said Seth implacably, and she bit her lip in impotent
fury.

There was no point in arguing with him now. There
wasn't much she could do this evening, anyway, but if
he thought that she was giving up without a fight he
would soon find that he was mistaken. She had all tonight to think about some way to persuade Winston to
take her to St Lucia. Once there, she could always say
that her passport had been stolen. The important thing
was to make sure that Tom got home as fast as possible.

Daisy's mind was working furiously. 'All right,' she
said. 'I'll stay. But I'm sleeping in the room next door.'

'Oh, no, you're not,' said Seth grimly. 'All the other
guests here think you're sleeping with me, and that's
what they're going to go on thinking.'

'They can think what they like,' snapped Daisy.
'They've all got their own private bungalows, and
they're not likely to creep around the house opening
doors, are they? Besides,' she added in a stinging voice,
'you're expected in Astra's bungalow tonight, and I
wouldn't want to cramp your style. I could do with a
night off, anyway.'

'A night off?' Seth's tone was dangerously quiet, but Daisy was too miserable to care.

'Given the number of nights we've spent together, I think you've had more than your money's worth, don't you?' Suddenly terrified that her precarious control was about to break, she flung her things into the case and marched to the door. Seth was still standing rigidly in the same place, and when she looked back his face was tight and somehow grey beneath his tan. 'I won't be coming to dinner,' she said. 'You can tell everyone that I've got a headache, if you care so much about what they think. I've had enough company today!'

It was the longest evening of Daisy's life. She lay on the bed in the room next door and stared numbly at the ceiling. The wonderful, invigorating anger had drained away, leaving her utterly empty. She could hear laughter and voices echoing down the corridor from the living-room. Obviously they weren't missing her; it sounded as if there was a full-scale party in progress. They wouldn't be carrying on like that if Seth wasn't there, surely? That meant that he must be smiling and talking as if nothing was wrong, perhaps taking the opportunity for a few private words with Astra under the cover of the general conversation.

Daisy tortured herself imagining them together—picturing every little touch, every look they exchanged—while the vicious claws of pain raked across her heart. If only she could cry. If only she could shout or scream or do anything. But it was as if her entire body had cramped and she could only lie curled desolately on the bed and stare at the plain white wall.

Grace had tapped on the door once, sounding worried and asking if she wanted anything to eat, but Daisy had simply told her that she wasn't hungry and after a while the housekeeper had gone away. After that she'd been left alone.

At long last the party in the living-room broke up. Daisy could hear them making their way to their bunga-lows, shouting loud goodnights or laughing idiotically over some private joke, but she was listening only for the sound of Seth opening the door of the room next to hers. It didn't come.

Daisy lay in the darkness and faced the truth. If Seth wasn't in his room there was only one other place he could be. He must have slipped quietly by to Astra's bungalow under the cover of everyone else's noise. He would be there now, his sure brown hands moving over Astra's skin and his warm mouth exploring hers. The very thought stabbed at Daisy, and the pain made her curl in on herself with a sharp intake of breath.

She should be thinking about Tom, Daisy told herself desperately. She should be thinking of a way to contact him; of a way to leave Cutlass Cay as soon as possible. She should be thinking of how Seth had used her and deceived her and made a fool out of her.

But all she could think about was how he had made love to her under the palms, while the hot wind soughed through the leaves overhead and the fringed shadows swayed over his body. Had it only been that day? The enchantment of the afternoon already belonged to the past—to a lifetime ago when she'd been happy.

The realisation of how utterly that happiness had gone crumbled the icy numbness around Daisy's heart at last, and she began to cry. In the darkness the hot, slow tears trickled silently down her cheeks, and she made no move to wipe them away.

The sun woke her the next morning. She had fallen into an exhausted sleep at last just before dawn, and the bright light striping through the shutters made her stir and reach for Seth. Her first reaction was a sense of panic at not finding him there. What was she doing sleeping alone in this strange room? As Daisy began to struggle up memory returned like a blow, and she sank back against the pillow as despair and desolation over-whelmed her.

It was only the thought of Tom that got her up in the end. Moving like an automaton, she dressed and tried to force her tired brain into activity. She had to contact Tom. She had to contact Tom. Repeating the phrase to herself like a mantra, Daisy put on a pair of sunglasses to hide her red, despairing eyes and went out into the corridor. If Winston wouldn't take her with him surely he would at least take a note for Tom?

There was no sign of Seth or, indeed, of anyone. It must be earlier than she had thought. The brightness of the day taunted Daisy, and she looked away from the familiar mint-green lagoon and the white glare of the beach. Grace was cleaning up the debris of the night before in the living-room when she found her. The housekeeper clicked her tongue in concern when she saw Daisy.

'You look terrible,' she said worriedly. 'Is everything all right?'

'I…had a migraine, that's all,' said Daisy with diffi-culty. 'Grace, could you find me some paper, please? I need to write a note to give to Winston.'

'Winston's gone,' said Grace in surprise, and Daisy sank down onto a chair.

'G-gone?'

'About an hour ago.' Grace looked at her closely. 'Are you sure you're all right?'

Daisy put a hand to her head. She needed to think! Winston had been her only way of contacting Tom, and

Seth knew it. He had deliberately sent Winston away out of her reach. Anger and frustration jostled with desolation and she got rather shakily to her feet. 'I think I'll go back to bed,' she said, needing to be on her own. 'If anyone asks would you just say that I'm not well?'

She spent the morning shut in the room while her mind circled frantically around her limited options, and her anger with Seth burned like a cold, steady flame inside her. When he rapped peremptorily on her door and entered without waiting for an answer Daisy didn't even look up.

'You're not going to skulk in here all day,' he grated. 'I know you're not sick. You can tell them all you've had a headache, if you like, but you're coming out to lunch right now.'

'I'm not hungry,' she said tonelessly.

'I don't care whether you're hungry or not—you're coming, and if I hear one suggestion from you that all is not well between us you'll find yourself dumped on the nearest island with no money, no passport and certainly no way of finding your precious Tom!'

Daisy had little choice but to go with him. Muttering something about a migraine, she sat at the table and pushed a salad around her plate while around her everyone discussed migraines *they* had had, each more agonising than the last. Seth took little part in the conversation. Outwardly he appeared much as usual, but his mouth was set in bleak line and a muscle hammered insistently in his jaw.

They had nearly finished by the time a commotion arose down at the jetty. Daisy was too wrapped up in her own misery and anger to take much notice at first but after a few minutes Grace came in and stood by the door, looking hesitant.

'What is it, Grace?' asked Seth.

'There's a young man just come in to the jetty in a launch,' said Grace. 'The gardener saw him coming and went down to tell him this is private, but he's refusing to leave.' She paused, and her eyes slid to where Daisy was sitting listlessly at the other end of the table. 'He says he won't go until he's seen Miss Daisy.'

Daisy lifted her head at that. 'He wants to see *me*?'

'That's what he says.'

Pushing back her chair, Daisy got to her feet and went out onto the verandah. A stocky, fair-haired young man was standing down on the jetty, his square jaw thrust aggressively forward as the gardener blocked his way. Daisy stopped dead, and closed her eyes. It couldn't be… When she opened them he was still there and she moved jerkily, stumbling down the steps and beginning to run towards him.

'Tom! Oh, *Tom*! Thank God you've come!'

CHAPTER TEN

'OH, TOM, I'm so glad to see you!' Daisy threw herself into her stepbrother's arms and burst into overwrought tears. 'I've been trying to find you for ages!'

'Hey, come on, Sis!' Tom patted his distraught stepsister awkwardly on the back, evidently unprepared for such an emotional welcome. 'There's no need to cry. I'm here now.' He seemed to hear her words for the first time. 'And what's this about trying to find me? I've been trying to find *you*!'

'*Me*?' Raising her head from his shoulder, she stared at him in astonishment. 'How on earth did you know that *I* was here?'

'I read some ludicrous article about you being in love with Seth Carrington,' said Tom. 'It was syndicated in one of the papers here, and it was pure chance that I saw it at all. I couldn't believe it when I saw your picture! It just seemed utterly fantastic... I mean, you and *Seth Carrington*!' An expression of concern creased Tom's square, handsome face.

'I suppose you know what you're doing, Daisy? You've always been such an innocent, and Seth Carrington's got a very unpleasant reputation. I've heard a lot about him since I've been out here and, by all accounts, he's not a man you want to tangle with at all. When I read that you were coming out here with him...well, I thought I ought to check that you were all right. Fortunately you weren't too far away, and eventually I managed to borrow this boat off a mate of mine.'

He nodded at the rather shabby motor launch that was

tied up to the jetty behind him and then hesitated, looking a little shamefaced. 'And, to tell you the truth, Daisy,
I wanted to find out if Dad was OK. We had a terrible
row just before I left and I guess we both said things we
shouldn't have. I've been wanting to get in touch, but
thought you might be able to tell me if I'd been forgiven
or not. You know how stiff-necked Dad can be sometimes.'

'Not as far as you're concerned,' said Daisy tearfully.
'He's missed you terribly, Tom.' Then she told him just
how ill his father was, and how much he wanted to see
him again. 'Please say you'll go home as soon as you
can, Tom. Jim needs you now.'

'Of course I will.' Tom looked so devastated by the
news that it was Daisy's turn to put her arms round him,
and they hugged each other in wordless comfort. 'But
what about you, Daisy?' he said after a while. 'Are you
coming with me?'

Daisy bit her lip. 'It depends on Seth.' Even saying
his name hurt at the moment.

'What's it got to do with him?' said Tom with a touch
of belligerence. 'He can't stop you if you want to leave.'

'It's…it's rather difficult to explain,' she said hesitantly. How could she make Tom understand about the
deal she had made with Seth; about the bitterness and
the anger and the memories of heart-stopping joy that
bound her to him still?

Tom stared at her expression. 'You're not really in
love with him, are you?' he demanded incredulously. 'I
thought that story was just a bit of gossip blown out of
all proportion by the papers.'

'It was,' said Daisy with an edge of desperation.
'Look, I can't explain it all now, Tom. I'll go and tell
Seth that I have to leave right now.'

'Shall I come with you?'

'No,' she said quickly. If Tom saw the contemptuous way Seth treated her things might really turn nasty. 'It would be better for me to talk to him alone. You wait on the boat, and I'll be back as soon as I can.'

'All right,' Tom agreed reluctantly. 'Just yell if Carrington gives you any trouble,' he added darkly.

As she walked past the dining-room door Daisy could see the other guests still ensconced around the table, but Seth's chair was hidden behind the door and she had no way of telling whether he was there or not. She would get her things first, and then go in search of him.

In the event, Seth came to find her. Steeling herself against the memories, Daisy was back in the room with the big bed and the blissful memories—hastily throwing the few things she had brought with her into a case. She was just closing it when Seth opened the door abruptly. After everything he had said and done her heart still lurched at the sight of him, slamming so painfully against her ribs that it hurt to breathe.

Seth closed the door behind him. His face was set, his eyes stony. Crossing the room, he tossed her passport and an envelope onto the top of her case where they landed with a slap. 'You'll want these,' he said.

Daisy picked them up with shaking hands. 'You mean I can go?'

'After that touching little scene I just witnessed down at the jetty there doesn't seem much point in trying to convince anyone that you're in love with me any more, does there?' said Seth in a voice that cut her to the core. 'If anyone asks I'll say that you had bad news from home and, no doubt, I'll be assured by everyone that I'm well out of an unsuitable relationship. It must have been pretty obvious that you weren't ever going to fit in. I wouldn't have needed you for much longer, anyway,' he went on with the same stinging indifference. 'Astra's ready to sign the pre-nuptial contract so we can go public as soon as her divorce comes through.'

'I see,' said Daisy dully. Unable to look at Seth, she opened the envelope. It was full of crisp American hundred-dollar notes.

'I thought you'd prefer cash,' said Seth with a contemptuous look. 'You can count it if you want to, but you'll find that it's what we agreed—plus a bonus for being so much more convincing in bed than out of it. I felt it was the least you'd expect for all those extra services you rendered so effectively.'

Daisy went white. Those long hours of sweetness they had shared...the desire and the delight and golden enchantment...reduced to *services*? Mechanically she tucked the flap back into the envelope. 'I don't need to count it,' she said in a voice devoid of all emotion.

Picking up the suitcase, she walked back down the corridor. It was like walking through a nightmare. Putting one foot in front of another required an enormous effort of concentration, while every instinct in her body was screaming at her to turn around and walk into Seth's arms and beg him to let her stay. She could feel Seth just behind her, but they didn't exchange a word.

Grace came out of the dining-room just as Daisy passed, and her round face creased with surprise and then dismay as she took in the suitcase. 'Miss Daisy!' she exclaimed. 'What's wrong? It's not bad news, is it?'

'Yes,' said Seth curtly. 'She's going home.'

Grace looked so upset that Daisy dropped the suitcase and gave the housekeeper a hug. 'Goodbye, Grace,' she said, choking back the tears. 'Thank you for everything.'

'Oh, Miss Daisy...' Grace hugged her back. 'You make sure and come back soon!'

But she wouldn't be back. Daisy went out onto the verandah and down the steps into the harsh midday glare. She would never be back. She would never hear the insects whirring frantically in the darkness or distant sound of the waves breaking against the reef. She would never wake up to the sun slanting in through the shutters, or curl her toes into the soft white sand beneath the coconut palms. Never again would she float on her back in the lagoon, cocooned in sunlight and warmth and happiness.

She would never see Seth again. Never run her hands over his sleek, hard body; never feel him smile against her skin.

Never again.

Daisy faltered and half turned as the impossibility of it hit her at last. Seth had stopped at the bottom of the verandah steps, his expression implacable. Only the pounding muscle in his jaw moved at all in his face. 'Goodbye,' she said in a voice that cracked.

What did she expect him to do? Drag her back into his arms? Carry her back up the steps and along to the cool bedroom and tell her that he loved her?

'Goodbye,' was all he said.

He was letting her go. He was going to stand and watch her walk down to the jetty and out of his life. Daisy searched his face for a last-minute reprieve but his eyes were pitiless, and there was nothing she could do but turn her back and walk slowly, stiffly away.

The lagoon shimmered greenly through her tears and the jetty was no more than a blur, but somehow she made it along to the motor launch. Tom was waiting for her. He took her case and tossed it into the boat. Jumping down, he held up his hand to help her down. In spite of herself, Daisy hesitated and glanced back at the verandah. It wasn't too late. Seth could still call out; could still beckon her back...but he was just standing there by steps in the bright light, watching her leave.

She took Tom's hand and climbed down into the boat and out of sight. The engine shuddered into life, settling into a steady throb as Tom reversed away from the jetty. When he was clear he swung the boat round, guiding it carefully through a gap in the reef and out into the deep, dark blue sea. For a moment they seemed to pause there, and then he shoved the throttle forward and, with a great roar, the boat leapt ahead and out towards the empty, glittering horizon.

Daisy didn't look back, but when Tom glanced across at her he saw that the tears were pouring silently down her cheeks.

The journey back to England was a silent one. Tom was obviously preoccupied with thoughts about his sick father. Daisy knew that she should be comforting and reassuring him, but she felt as if she was struggling through a thick fog of misery and it was all she could do to keep herself together. She held herself so rigid against the pain of leaving Seth that every muscle in her body ached, but she knew that if she gave in to it she would simply shatter into a thousand icy pieces like her poor, splintered heart.

She hadn't know that it was possible to hurt this badly but Jim's face, when Tom walked into his room, made it impossible to regret what she had done. Once all the excitement had died down and they were preparing to leave Jim to rest, he called Daisy back. He took her hand and held it tightly.

'I don't have the words to thank you, Daisy,' he said a little unsteadily. 'Seeing Tom again and clearing up that stupid argument has meant more to me than I can possibly explain.'

Daisy's eyes stung with sudden tears. 'You don't have to thank me, Jim,' she said. 'Just get better.'

'I will.' Jim was looking tired, but there was a new confidence about him. 'This time I really think I will.'

Jim did get better. Slowly, surely—against all the doctors' predictions—his condition improved, until the day arrived that none of them had ever expected to see and he was allowed to leave hospital.

'I didn't think I'd ever be this happy again,' Ellen told Daisy that evening. Jim still tired easily, and Tom was helping him upstairs to bed. 'Jim's home and Tom told me that he's back to stay this time.'

'Is he?' Things had got rather chaotic at the flower shop during her absence, and Daisy had been so busy that she hadn't had any time for a private talk with Tom recently.

'He only left to protest at the way Jim was forcing him into the family business, but he said he was getting sick of knocking around doing odd jobs. I think he's ready to settle down at last. He's already been into the firm to start learning the ropes.' Ellen beamed. 'Jim's over the moon, and so am I. Tom and I had a long chat the other day and he told me that he only resented me for a few months after Jim and I were married. He was horrified when I told him that I thought that he and Jim had quarrelled about me.'

'I hope you believed him,' said Daisy, forcing a smile.

'Oh, yes,' sighed her mother contentedly. 'In fact, everything's worked out perfectly! We can all be happy now, can't we?'

Daisy looked out of the window. 'Yes,' she said flatly. It was a soft summer evening and the golden light dappled through the plane trees opposite, but all she could see were fringed palms etched sharply against a brilliant blue sky and sunlight spangling a shallow lagoon. Was Seth there now, lying with Astra in the shade and running his hand down her smooth, brown back? Did he ever think of her? Did he remember?

She tried not to think about him, but it was like trying not to breathe. The first agony had subsided to a dull, nagging ache inside her that would flare abruptly into excruciating pain at an unwary memory.

Sometimes Daisy felt as if that ache was all that existed. She had hoped that that terrible empty, desolate feeling would lessen as she got back into her routine, but it only got worse. It was no use telling herself that it would have ended like this anyway. Seth and she were two completely different people, with completely different lives. For a few short weeks they had been together, but it had been a time out of time—nothing to do with real life. A fantasy, that was all it had been. Why couldn't she just accept that?

Daisy had tried logic; she had tried reason; she had tried talking sternly to herself, but none of it worked. No matter what she did she was left with one inescapable fact: she was still in love with Seth, and she always would be. Every night she lay in her lonely bed and wondered if she was going to go through life feeling bereft without him. It was impossible to imagine a time when this dull ache of loss would lessen and her raw heart would heal.

It hurt to think about him, but it hurt even more not to know how he was and what he was doing. Daisy tortured herself by looking through the gossip columns, dreading the day when she would read about Astra's divorce or see a picture of her smiling next to Seth but desperate for any contact with him, however remote.

She had been back a month, and still there was no news of him in the papers. The gossip columns would have had a field day at the merest suspicion of a marriage between Seth Carrington and Astra Bentingger, and

Daisy was convinced that she couldn't have missed it. The continuing silence puzzled her. Astra had made it very plain that she was ready to get a divorce so what were they waiting for? The constant expectation of seeing the announcement was fraying Daisy's nerves, and although she made an effort when she was at home with Jim and her mother the rest of the time she was edgy and irritable and miserable.

Summer was always a hectic time in the shop and Daisy welcomed the pressure that gave her little time to think during the day, but it didn't make the nights any easier. That was when the memories would come crowding painfully in, and she would ache for Seth—for the touch of him and the taste of him and the feel of his sure hands on her body.

She would screw up her eyes tightly and pray that when she opened them again she would find herself back in the wide bed beneath the gauzy mosquito net with the moonlight shining through the shutters and the insects whirring and clicking in the dark tropical air. So vivid was the memory that Daisy would roll over and reach for Seth, only to realise that he wasn't there, and she would open her eyes to the desolate darkness of her empty room—to streetlight instead of moonlight, and the constant grumble of traffic instead of the sounds of a tropical night.

Things were so busy in the shop that Ellen came back for three days a week. In spite of Daisy's efforts, she was concerned about the fine-drawn lines of tension around her daughter's eyes. Daisy was a muted version of her previous self and had lost the sparkle and vitality which had always been so much part of her, but when Ellen tried to find out what was wrong she simply shook her head. 'I'm fine,' was all she would say.

* * *

It was another hot summer afternoon. Daisy was in the back of the shop, listlessly putting the finishing touches to a birthday bouquet and trying not to think about how different it was to the flowers she had gathered at Cutlass Cay. It was a relief to be on her own for a while and not have to remember to smile. Lisa was out delivering bouquets and her mother was at the front with one of their regular clients. Mrs Gregory's daughter was getting married at long last, after several years of resistance, and they were engaged in an animated discussion about flowers for the marquee.

The bell over the door jangled as Daisy was cutting a piece of ribbon to tie around the bouquet. She hoped that her mother would deal with whoever it was, but evidently Mrs Gregory was not to be deflected in full flow. 'Daisy!' called Ellen, and then added pleasantly to the new customer, 'She won't keep you a moment.'

Daisy sighed. Scissors and ribbon still in her hand, she went out through the bead curtain and saw who was standing on the other side of the counter.

Her heart stopped, and for an agonising moment it seemed as if it would never start again. Shock had driven the air from her lungs, along with all feeling, and she had the oddest sensation of being quite empty before instinctive joy blazed through her, followed by a great whoosh of feeling that kick-started her heart back into life. It was as if the wildly spinning world had stopped with a sickening jolt, leaving Daisy jarred and breathless and giddy.

'Hello,' said Seth. His face was thinner than she remembered and there was an oddly uncertain look in his eyes, but it was unmistakably him. She wanted to reach out and touch him to convince herself that he was real, but the bitterness of memory was already swamping that first unthinking burst of joy at the sight of him.

'What are you doing here?' she asked instead, and her voice sounded high and strange to her own ears.

'Daisy!' exclaimed Ellen in shock, but Seth didn't even notice. If Daisy hadn't known him better she would have said that he was at a loss as he glanced around him.

'I'd like some flowers,' he said, and she could have sworn that it was the first thing that came into his head.

Her fingers were gripping the scissors so tightly that the metal dug into her skin. What was Seth doing here—taunting her with his presence like this? It took an enormous effort not to dissolve in a puddle of longing at his feet, but she was determined not to let him make a fool of her again. If he wanted to play this game she would play it the way he wanted.

'You can see what we have,' she said tightly, nodding her head at the buckets of long-stemmed roses and sunflowers, delphiniums and daisies, sweet peas and iris. 'Choose whatever you want.'

'I'd like you to choose for me,' said Seth. 'I'd like a bouquet.'

Daisy's face was like stone. 'What sort of bouquet?' Out of the corner of her eye she could see her mother turn with a frown at her tone, but she didn't care. She had longed and longed to see Seth again, but she hadn't realised that it would hurt so much.

'The most romantic one you can put together,' he told her, without taking his eyes from her face. 'I don't care how much it costs. I want to give it to the girl I love.'

Why was he doing this to her? Daisy wanted to scream and shout, but Mrs Gregory was still yapping on to her mother and there was nothing for it but to move stiffly round the counter and begin selecting blooms. Some perverse sense of pride made her determined to make the most beautiful bouquet to prove to him that she didn't care. Her head was bent over the sweetly scented buckets of flowers, but she was very conscious of Seth watching her in silence.

Her hands were unsteady as she arranged the flowers with some foliage and wrapped them in Cellophane. Even in a state of shock her eye was unerring, and the finished effect of varying hues of blue and pink, haloed by the white blur of gypsophilia, was exquisite. Daisy looked down at the bouquet and felt tears grip her throat before she forced them down. She wouldn't cry in front of Seth. She *wouldn't*.

Stiffening her spine, she turned and laid the bouquet on the counter. 'How much is that?' asked Seth, without even looking at it. When Daisy told him he handed over a credit card. Her fingers fumbled as she tried to fit the card and voucher into the machine and then, of course, she had to fill out the voucher, but her writing was so shaky that it was practically illegible. It seemed to take ages, but eventually Seth had signed it and she had handed him back his card and receipt.

'Thank you,' he said formally, tucking them into his wallet and slipping it back into the inside pocket of his linen jacket. He picked up the bouquet.

She couldn't hold back the tears any longer. Unable to watch him leave, Daisy muttered a goodbye and blundered back through the bead curtain to sink down into a chair and cover her face with her hands as she gave in and cried at long last.

There was a soft step outside and then a ripple of clicks as the bead curtain was brushed aside. 'Why are you crying, Daisy?' asked Seth's voice.

'I'm not crying,' she sobbed.

'All right, why aren't you crying?'

Daisy stiffened at the suspicious note of amusement just threading his voice. 'It's noting to do with you,' she wept, sounding rather muffled through her fingers. 'Go away!'

'I'm not going to go until I've given you this,' said Seth firmly and Daisy lowered her hands, to see him holding out the bouquet.

'I don't want Astra's flowers!' she said, scrubbing the tears from her face with the back of her hand.

'I didn't buy them for Astra,' he said. 'I bought them for the girl I'm in love with.' He paused. 'I bought them for you, Daisy.'

There was a long, long silence. Daisy stared at the flowers, hardly daring to believe what she had heard. 'For me?' she whispered at last.

'For you.'

Very slowly she raised her eyes. The grey gaze held an anxious expression that set her heart thumping in incredulous hope. 'But...but you're going to marry Astra.'

'No, I'm not,' said Seth. 'I thought I wanted to a long time ago—before I met you and realised what it was to fall in love. I was so sure that I never would,' he went on slowly, without taking his eyes from Daisy's. 'I'd seen love devalued and demeaned so often when I was growing up that I'd decided that I didn't want anything to do with it, but what my parents called love was nothing to do with the way I felt whenever I looked into those brave blue eyes of yours. I told myself that *that* wasn't love either; that wanting to touch you and hold you was no more than physical desire, but whenever I saw another man—like James Gifford-Gould—so much as look at you I wanted to kill him.'

'You couldn't have been in love with me,' said Daisy involuntarily. 'You were so horrible to me!'

'I know I was.' Seth's smile was rather twisted. 'I was rude and arrogant and all those things you said I was. I was furious with myself for letting myself fall in love with you. As far as I was concerned, you were just a cheap actress—and that was probably just a grand name for how you really made your living—but your eyes were so clear and your kisses so sweet that I was utterly confused. A cheap actress was what I had wanted—that's why I approached Dee Pearce—but I didn't want you to be like that.

'I found myself pretending that you were only interested in me, and then I'd catch myself up and realise that I was well on the way to making a complete fool of myself. You'd never made any secret of what you did, or what you wanted, and there I was—considering throwing up all my careful plans for you! I'd never been so unsure of myself before, and I'm afraid I took it out on you.' He paused. 'I haven't given you any reason to love me, I know, Daisy. I wouldn't blame you if you said you never wanted to see me again.'

He was still holding the flowers, their soft, pretty colours contrasting with his hard, masculine lines. 'So, why did you come here today?' asked Daisy unsteadily. She had risen to her feet and was holding onto the back of the chair for support.

'Because I had to tell you how I felt. Because I knew that I would never be quite happy again unless you were with me. Because I couldn't stop remembering those long nights we spent together, and I hoped that you would remember them too.' Seth stopped and looked across at Daisy, whose eyes were huge and dark in her thin face. '*Do* you remember, Daisy?' he asked softly.

Remember? Remember the hot, tropical nights? Remember the touch of his hands and the feel of his body and the soaring, spinning joy they had discovered together? 'Yes,' she said huskily. 'I remember.'

Her gaze fell to the bouquet Seth held. For the first time she noticed that he was gripping the stems so tightly

that they were crushed and bruised. There was something about the sight of his white, tense knuckles that
broke through the barrier of numb disbelief at last, and
she saw not the arrogant, assured tycoon but a man who
was anxious and uncertain and mentally bracing himself
for defeat.

'Are those flowers really for me?' she asked slowly.

'Yes.' Seth seemed to be having as much difficulty
speaking as Daisy.

'You really love me?'

He nodded. 'Yes,' he said again, and she held out her
hands.

'I'd better take them, then,' she said.

Mechanically Seth handed them over and Daisy
smiled at last. 'Thank you,' she said and stepped towards
him to kiss him very gently on the cheek. At the touch
of her lips Seth's careful control snapped, and his arms
came round her to pull her fiercely against him so that
he could bury his face in her dark curls.

'Daisy…' he muttered desperately. 'Daisy, tell me you
love me.'

'I love you,' she said, half laughing, half crying,
oblivious to the flowers which had been irredeemably
crushed between them. 'Of course I love you.'

Seth released his grip on her only enough to lift his
head and look down into her face. 'Really?' he asked
wonderingly.

'Really, really,' she said, her blue eyes still starry with
tears.

'So you'll come back to me? You'll marry me?'

'Yes, yes…oh, *yes*!' said Daisy, and he kissed her at
last.

Dizzy with longing and relief, they clung together almost frantically. It was a long, long kiss which left them
both breathless and shaken. 'Let's get rid of these

damned flowers,' said Seth unsteadily at last, tossing the bouquet carelessly aside and drawing Daisy close against him once more. He laid his cheek against her silky hair. 'I've missed you so much, Daisy. I didn't know how much I loved you until I saw you throw yourself into Tom's arms that day, and I knew it was too late to tell you. I had to stand and watch that boat, taking you away from me.' His arms tightened around her. 'That was the worst day of my life.'

'I had to go,' said Daisy, her voice muffled against his throat. 'I had to make sure Tom got home.'

'I know, darling. If I hadn't been such a pig-headed fool I would have let you tell me about Tom a long time ago, and I could have spared myself a month of sheer hell. As it was, I was so devastated when you left that I couldn't talk to anyone. I told Astra and the others that they could stay if they wanted to, but I was going back to New York. I thought it would be easier to be somewhere I hadn't known you, but it wasn't. It was worse. I stuck it out for nearly three weeks before giving in and going back to Cutlass Cay. I'd tried telling myself that I'd get over you soon enough and that hadn't worked, so I wanted to be somewhere where I felt closer to you.'

He kissed Daisy's hair with a rueful smile. 'Grace soon sorted me out. She wanted to know how I could have been stupid enough to let you go, and she was the one who told me that Tom was your brother. I didn't know whether to be overjoyed or appalled at how foolish I'd been!'

'I should have tried harder to tell you,' said Daisy, prepared to forgive him anything now.

'I wouldn't have listened,' said Seth. 'I was too jealous. I'd taken you off to Cutlass Cay to have you all to myself, only to find that you were looking for another man. You'd suggested that we make the most of the time

we had together and I told myself that was all I was
doing, but I couldn't bear to even think of you with
anyone else. I knew I couldn't refuse to let you go but,
when Winston found Tom with his typical efficiency, I
couldn't resist keeping you with me just a few days
longer so I didn't tell you.'

He tipped Daisy's head back gently and wiped the last
tear-stains from her face with unsteady thumbs. 'I'm
sorry, darling,' he said. 'Do you think your stepfather
will ever forgive me for the delay in seeing Tom again?'

'He will when he sees how happy I am,' sighed Daisy,
snuggling into the hard security of his body. All those
bitter nights of thinking that she would never see Seth
again and now he was here, holding her, touching her.
'This isn't a dream, is it?' she asked, suddenly assailed
by doubts, and she felt him smile against her hair.

'If it is we're sharing it together.'

They were silent for a moment, content just to hold
each other and let the misery and the tension seep slowly
away. 'What about Astra?' asked Daisy, stirring at last
and looking up into Seth's face.

'Haven't you heard? She's decided that she likes being married to Dimitrios after all, and they've just announced that she's expecting a baby.'

Daisy was flabbergasted. 'But...but she wants to
marry *you*!'

'Not any more, she doesn't.' Seth grinned at her expression. 'Astra always likes to keep her options open.
That's why she dickered so long over the pre-nuptial
contract. It's why she suddenly appeared at Cutlass Cay
as well. We'd agreed to let everything drop for a while,
and although I told you she was coming out to give me
an excuse for taking you, I hadn't said any more to
Astra. It was always more of a business arrangement
than anything else, but Astra obviously suspected that

one of her options was closing off when she read that article about how much in love we were. She knew that I wasn't *that* good an actor.

'I guess she realised as soon as she saw us together that it was all true, but Astra never gives up without a fight. She did everything she could to try and divide us.'

'She succeeded,' said Daisy soberly, and told Seth how Astra had tried to persuade her to leave in exchange for the diamond bracelet. 'I was convinced that you'd been discussing me with her and, then, when you didn't sleep in your room that night I was so sure that you'd gone to her.'

'You thought I was with Astra—after the day we'd spent together? Seth pretended to shake her. 'Daisy, how could you even *begin* to think something like that?'

'Well, where *were* you?'

'On the beach,' he said. 'I couldn't face getting into that damned bed without you. I spent most of the night sitting on the sand trying to convince myself that I'd be better off without you, and only succeeded in wanting you more than ever.'

'Oh, Seth, we've wasted so much time!' said Daisy, but he was drawing her across to the sagging armchair in the corner and pulling her down into his lap.

'We'll make up for it,' he promised, and for a long time all else was forgotten but the blissful happiness of long, deep, sweet kisses that slowly dissolved the memories of the achingly lonely nights they had spent apart.

'I've been so unhappy,' Daisy sighed at last, mumbling kisses against his ear, his temple, his hair—anywhere that she could reach—while his lips were travelling lovingly along her jaw. 'I kept waiting to see the news of your marriage to Astra. She told me that she was about to get a divorce.'

'She told me that too,' said Seth. 'At the time that she

told me that she'd bought you off. She seemed to think that I'd be pleased at getting rid of a potentially embarrassing "entanglement", as she called you. It took me some time to convince her that I had no intention of marrying her any longer. As far as I was concerned, the deal had been off ever since she'd instructed her lawyers to put the contract negotiations on hold.

'It didn't go down very well,' he added with a rueful grin. 'Astra's not used to being refused. She told me that I was mad to give up the chance of an alliance with her and couldn't believe that I would turn down such a fantastic deal just because of you, but when she realised that I wasn't going to change my mind she obviously decided that she'd be better off going back to Dimitrios.'

Daisy's arms had been wrapped around his neck, but now she sat back slightly. 'Are you sure you're doing the right thing, Seth?' she asked hesitantly, fiddling with his tie. '*Wouldn't* it be a fantastic deal?'

'The only deal I want is with you,' said Seth, removing her hands firmly from his tie and planting a kiss in each palm. 'I could make all the alliances I liked, but none of them would mean anything unless you were with me. I've learnt that this last month. I feel lopsided without you now, Daisy. When you're not there there's an empty space beside me that only you can fill.' The grey eyes smiling into hers were warmer than Daisy had ever dreamt they could be. 'I can do without Astra's millions,' he told her, 'but I can't do without your warmth and your smile or knowing that if I reach out at night you'll be there.'

His eyes told Daisy everything she needed to know and she relaxed back against him. 'I'll be there as long as you want me,' she said simply.

'Then you'll be there for ever,' said Seth, releasing

her hands to tangle his fingers in her hair and draw her mouth back towards his.

'Shall we put it in the pre-nuptial contract?' teased Daisy against his lips.

'We won't need one of those,' he told her between kisses. 'There's only one thing we need to agree on, and that's that I'm never letting you go again—and I'm afraid I'm not open to negotiation on that!'

'Oh, well,' she pretended to sigh, slipping her arms back round his neck. 'If those are your conditions I suppose I'm just going to have to accept!'

Much, much later—when Ellen had put her head through the bead curtain, raised her brows at the sight of her daughter wrapped blissfully in Seth's arms and tactfully retired again—Daisy emerged from another long kiss with a deep, shuddering breath of sheer joy.

'How did you find me?' she asked belatedly, resting her head back against his shoulder where it felt so right and proper.

'With great difficulty.' Seth smoothed a wayward curl away from her face. 'It was terrible to realise how little I really knew about you. I couldn't find you in the phone book and then I realised that you might be living with your mother and stepfather, in which case you'd be listed under Johnson—do you know how many of *them* there are in the London directory? Then I had a bit of luck. A friend of mine in New York said that a friend of his had a stunning new girlfriend called Dee Pearce, and of course I remembered that she was a friend of yours.'

'Ah,' said Daisy apprehensively. She had forgotten that she had never told Seth the truth about how they had met. She peeked a glance at him under her lashes, but although he was trying to look severe he couldn't help laughing.

'Is that all you can say?' he teased. 'I managed to get

hold of Dee on her own eventually and we had a very confusing conversation—until I established that she'd never had a letter from me and had certainly never had a friend called Daisy Deare. But she did say that her letters were often delivered to Lawrence Street instead of Lawrence Crescent, and vice versa, and after that everything fell into place.'

'I did try and take your letter round to her,' Daisy said a little defensively. 'I'd opened it by mistake, and I thought the least I could do was explain. Then, when I heard that she'd gone away, it seemed somehow *meant* that I should pretend to be her. I was desperate to find Tom.' A thought struck her. 'Was she livid with me for doing her out of a job?'

Seth shook his head. 'She's very happy with this guy she's got at the moment, and hoping it might prove permanent, so she wouldn't have been interested anyway.'

'That's a relief.' Daisy kissed the pulse below his ear, the very spot where she had first kissed him when she'd been trying to convince him that she was an actress after all. 'We ought to write and thank the Post Office, Seth,' she sighed happily. 'If they hadn't delivered your letter to the wrong address we might never have met.' She shivered at the thought and Seth tightened his arms around her.

'You can write, if you want,' he said, 'but personally I don't think it had anything to do with the Post Office. You and I were meant for each other, Daisy Deare, and that letter was directed by destiny!'

MILLS & BOON®

Next Month's Romances

Each month you can choose from a wide variety of romance novels from Mills & Boon. Below are the new titles to look out for next month from the Presents and Enchanted series.

Presents™

AN IDEAL MARRIAGE?	Helen Bianchin
SECOND MARRIAGE	Helen Brooks
TIGER, TIGER	Robyn Donald
SEDUCING NELL	Sandra Field
MISTRESS AND MOTHER	Lynne Graham
HUSBAND NOT INCLUDED!	Mary Lyons
THE LOVE-CHILD	Kathryn Ross
THE RANCHER'S MISTRESS	Kay Thorpe

Enchanted™

TAMING A HUSBAND	Elizabeth Duke
BARGAINING WITH THE BOSS	Catherine George
BRANNIGAN'S BABY	Grace Green
WAITING FOR MR WONDERFUL	Stephanie Howard
THE WAY TO A MAN'S HEART	Debbie Macomber
NO ACCOUNTING FOR LOVE	Eva Rutland
GEORGIA AND THE TYCOON	Margaret Way
KIT AND THE COWBOY	Rebecca Winters

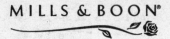

MILLS & BOON®

In Sultry New Orleans,
Passion and Scandal are...

Unmasked

Mills & Boon are delighted to bring you a star studded
line-up of three internationally renowned authors in one
compelling volume—

Janet Dailey
Elizabeth Gage
Jennifer Blake

Set in steamy, sexy New Orleans, this fabulous collection of
three contemporary love stories centres around one magical
night—the annual masked ball.

Disguised as legendary lovers, the elite of New Orleans are
seemingly having the times of their lives.
Guarded secrets remain hidden—until midnight...
when *everyone* must unmask...

Available: August 1997   Price: £4.99

FREE!

FOUR FREE
specially selected
Enchanted™ novels
PLUS a FREE Mystery Gift
when you return this page...

Return this coupon and we'll send you 4 Mills & Boon® Enchanted™ novels and a mystery gift absolutely FREE! We'll even pay the postage and packing for you.

We're making you this offer to introduce you to the benefits of the Reader Service™– FREE home delivery of brand-new Mills & Boon Enchanted novels, at least a month before they are available in the shops, FREE gifts and a monthly Newsletter packed with information, competitions, author profiles and lots more...

Accepting these FREE books and gift places you under no obligation to buy, you may cancel at any time, even after receiving just your free shipment. Simply complete the coupon below and send it to:

MILLS & BOON READER SERVICE, FREEPOST, CROYDON, SURREY, CR9 3WZ.

READERS IN EIRE PLEASE SEND COUPON TO PO BOX 4546, DUBLIN 24

NO STAMP NEEDED

Yes, please send me 4 free Enchanted novels and a mystery gift. I understand that unless you hear from me, I will receive 6 superb new titles every month for just £2.20* each, postage and packing free. I am under no obligation to purchase any books and I may cancel or suspend my subscription at any time, but the free books and gift will be mine to keep in any case. (I am over 18 years of age)

N7YE

Ms/Mrs/Miss/Mr_____
BLOCK CAPS PLEASE

Address_____

_____

_____ Postcode _____

ERICA SPINDLER

Bestselling Author of *Forbidden Fruit*

FORTUNE

BE CAREFUL WHAT YOU WISH FOR...
IT JUST MIGHT COME TRUE

Skye Dearborn's wishes seem to be coming true, but will Skye's new life prove to be all she's dreamed of—or a nightmare she can't escape?

"A high adventure of love's triumph over twisted obsession."

—*Publishers Weekly*

"Give yourself plenty of time, and enjoy!"

—*Romantic Times*